PRINCE OF RUINS

BOOK 1

KEVIN MACKLIN

SCIENCE FICTION FANTASY
FOR THE CULTURE
W. CLARK PUBLISHING

Wahida Clark Presents Innovative Publishing
60 Evergreen Place
Suite 904A
East Orange, New Jersey 07018
1(866) 910-6920
www.wclarkpublishing.com

Library of Congress Cataloging-In-Publication Data:
Prince of Ruins
Paperback ISBN 978-1-954161-75-7
Hardback ISBN 978-1-954161-88-7
eBook ISBN 978-1-954161-76-4
LCCN: 2021925596

1. Action-packed Thrill Ride 2. Post-apocalyptic 3. Sci-fi Books with Black Characters 4. Military Sci-fi Thriller 5. African Fantasy 6. African American Post-apocalyptic 7. Sci-fi Books with Royalty 8. Fantasy Books with Black Royals 9. Sci-fi Books with Black Main Characters 10. African American Science Fiction
Creative Direction by Nuance Art LLC
Cover design by Tina Shivers
Layout by Caroline Zonis
Printed in United States

This book is dedicated to everyone who has been in need of a second chance.

ACKNOWLEDGMENTS

I would like to thank Wahida Clark, Chase Bolling and the entire SF/F for the Culture team. You believed in me and hopefully I delivered to your expectations. A special thanks to my mom, Carla Macklin. My day one. Ty Parks, remember when I was making a podcast and you said I should put it on Amazon. Without you this wouldn't exist. Nakia Burris, you always asking me when I'm going to start writing again keeps me writing. Brittni Johnson, your pop ups bout to be lit! Let's sell some books. Chris, Rock, Dre, Michelle, Shakina, BJ, AJ... I love y'all. Mark, I miss you, fam. Rest easy. There are countless others that are unnamed. You know what it is! Love!

PART I

NNENDI

1944

The earth shook as shells exploded against the wall. Hundreds of rifles tapped out a staccato melody as they were fired in quick succession. Repeatedly, without pause, it soon became the song that wouldn't end.

The tanks are the real problem, King Nnendi thought, as he worried over the wall's integrity. If the walls fell and the savages attacked his people, all would be lost.

Standing in the middle of the battle, Nnendi forced himself to relax, opening a rip to the spirit plane and focusing all of his energy toward his Champions. They wore Anokian inscribed, golden palm disks around their hands, allowing them to amplify and focus the King's power towards their enemy, turning that energy into a mighty weapon. Every time a soldier came into contact with the force, their bodies were overloaded with its energy, effectively short circuiting their systems and leaving them severely injured and sometimes dead.

But, the tanks were almost completely unaffected by the

force, and they were pummeling the city's wall with barrage after barrage of cannon fire.

A few soldiers of the attacking enemy force were able to break through the line of Champions and were met by the Gazania, a group of warrior women who were feared for their ferocity in battle. Stabbing with their bayonets, they were quickly cut down by the swords and spears of the fighting women, their long locks hanging down their backs.

Knocking down a large chunk of the wall, a shell from one of the tanks struck true, opening a large, V-shaped void above a fracture that ran all the way to the bottom of the wall.

With half of his mind in the spirit plane and the other half in the battle, King Nnendi noticed that one of his Champions, Ude, had broken ranks and was charging toward the enemy lines. Clearing a path though the enemy soldiers using the force, he made for one of the tanks as its turret turned to track him.

Circling to avoid the turret, Ude moved closer to the hulking tank. As he closed in, he saw that the force was beginning to bend the turret, and he continued until it was as twisted as a pretzel.

That's when the bombers came, diving low, their screaming engines causing the King's forces to stare skyward, with fear of the planes crashing prevalent amongst the ranks.

But, it was worse than that. Before pulling up and making for the heavens, the bombers released their payloads across the King's lines, as well as in the city.

Nnendi struggled to maintain his connection to the spirit plane as panic for the innocent people within the city's walls tugged at his concentration. He needed all the focus he could muster to power the Champion's weapons as they defended the front lines.

The bombs exploded all around him, their deafening song followed by the screams of the injured. Fires raged inside of the city as homes burned and buildings crumbled, crushing their cremated inhabitants.

Lowering their cannons, the tanks disengaged the wall and began firing at King Nnendi's warriors, the massive artillery ripping to pieces anyone they struck.

Following Ude's example, the remaining eleven Champions raced toward the tanks in suicidal fashion, but to stay in place was certain death as they waited to be decimated by the tanks' artillery.

Returning for their second run, the bombers rained death and destruction upon the King's forces, weakening their resistance enough for enemy soldiers to rush the field of battle as smoke from grass fires stung the eyes of both armies.

Gazania engaged the soldiers, experiencing a fair amount of success at first, but it was short lived. It was like a river of soldiers were flowing into the battlefield, unrestricted and without pause, and in the end there were just too many.

"Your Grace, we must retreat," said Kwame, captain of the King's personal guard as well as one of King Nnendi's oldest friends. "My job is to protect you, and I would be honored to give my life for yours. But, if we don't move, my life will be given in vain."

Nnendi was furious. These people would come to his land, attack his people, and all for what? His kingdom had offended no one!

"They will all die!" the King declared.

"Not if we're all dead first," Kwame tried to reason. "The people need you. Your power is the best weapon we have, and without you, the people have no hope."

Trying to maintain his connection to the spirit plane so his Champions could have a fighting chance, he turned to Kwame and said, "As always, you are right. Even if I don't want to listen. To the city, then."

Reaching the wall, the two men climbed the pile of rubble

at the base of a gaping hole that had been carved out by the bombers and entered the city.

"This way," Kwame said as he guided the King through the destruction that had once been his capital city.

Heavy with debris, the air was so polluted they couldn't see more than a few feet ahead as they dodged larger chunks of the wall that had been knocked off by the bombardment.

Reaching the palace, King Nnendi went straight for the Queen's chambers to retrieve his wife and son, who were huddled in a corner when he entered.

"You're okay," Queen Chiwendu exclaimed as she saw her husband.

"Barely. We must leave, immediately. Come," the King beckoned.

"I have to get-" she was interrupted as she turned to a door at the side of the room.

"No time. Come now!"

King Nnendi took his son in one hand, his Queen in the other, and ran out of the door where Kwame was waiting.

"This way, Your Grace," he said, leading them to the secret passage that hadn't seen use in hundreds of years.

After sliding the massive stone to the side, revealing the entrance, Kwame said, "Climb in."

Wife and child entered first, followed by King Nnendi who, after a few steps, turned back to his friend and said, "What are you doing? Come."

"Go, Your Grace. I'll be fine."

"As your King, I command you to get into this passage."

"Nnendi, as your oldest friend I'm telling you I've got this. Go! Get the Queen and Prince to safety!"

Climbing out of the passage, King Nnendi embraced his good friend, then without a word, climbed back into the passage and disappeared with his wife and child.

1

—————

JASON

Present

Clink...

Steel banged against steel as the door to my cell was first unlocked, then opened. I'd been asleep, lying on my back. The sharp noise immediately pulled me from the depths of dreamland, and I rose up onto my elbows. I Squinted into the light filtering through the open door.

Two shadowy silhouettes stood in the doorway.

This was highly unusual. It was the middle of the night, and I was in prison. Death row, to be exact. I'd been here for the past five years. In this same, small, eight by twelve cell. Waiting to die.

The last time I'd had a visitor was... well, never. I had no one. I was a loner. My family had been killed during the Z Wars. After, it was just hard to trust anyone.

And hard to let my guard down.

The world was decimated. Everyone had nothing. People were scrabbling to feed what was left of their families and themselves. Doing what was necessary to survive was commonplace. If you had bread, you had a friend. Or, someone trying to stab you in the back for it.

So, I trusted no one. And no one came to visit.

"Jason Alexander," the man said. It was definitely a statement. No way to accidentally stumble upon me by random chance.

He knew who I was, but I didn't know why he was here.

"What do you want?" I asked.

"You," he replied.

"I'm not sure what you mean..."

"What if I told you that you could walk out of here a free man? Tonight. Alive. No more waiting around for your number to be called. No more sitting around, looking at these same, drab four walls. What would you say to that?"

"I'd say to quit playing with me and get out of my cell so I can go back to sleep."

The man stepped further into my cell and turned toward my bunk. The light from outside played across the side of his face and I could finally make out his features. Sharp cheekbones, with a straight, narrow nose. Thin lips. His suit was dark and well fitted to his frame. My position on the bunk made it hard to judge his true height, but at the moment, he towered over me.

"I'm not messing with you." His voice was deep and warm, like he sang tenor in an acapella group and drank hot tea with honey every morning. "This could be a second chance."

"Why me? I don't understand." I sat up in my bunk, putting my feet on the cold floor. "Is everyone going free? Did some law change? What are you talking about?"

"This offer is only for you."

"Are you a lawyer?" I asked.

"No," he responded.

"Who are you?"

"Forgive my lack of courtesy. I'm Agent Mays of External Security. Pleased to meet you."

External Security was everything defense for the nation of Elan. It was the Army, Navy, Air Force, CIA, and Homeland Security all wrapped up into one entity. They kept Elan safe from all outside threats. They defended Elan's borders and fought Elan's wars.

What they *didn't* do was police the interior. I was on death row for an internal incident that had absolutely nothing to do with External Security. There was absolutely no reason for an agent of External Security to be standing in my cell, in the middle of the night, making an offer to free a man condemned to be executed for an internal matter.

"What's this offer you speak of?" I asked.

"We want you to do a job. The Nation of Elan *needs* you to do this job. It's a matter of national security."

"What, exactly, is this job?" I asked.

"As a matter of national security, I can't tell you what it is until you make a commitment. But, who cares what the job is? You'll be rewarded with your life. You'll get to breathe fresh air, instead of this moldy crap you've been sucking in for the past five years. You'll get to make decisions, move freely. Touch a woman, eh?" He winked as he said the last part. "What would that be worth to you? What would you not do for your own life?"

Agent Mays waved his arm around the small cell. "Obviously, you're willing to take a life. I know you don't have to think about it that hard."

His last jab got under my skin. Sure, I was here for killing someone. And some would agree that it was in defense of myself. Maybe not everyone. But, some.

I had gotten into a fight in a bar. More a brawl than a fight. But, there was this one particular guy who turned out to be a skilled fighter. Look, no one fights to lose. So, I rose to the challenge and grabbed a barstool. Swung it, connecting with the side of his head. I figured, at most, I'd knock him out for a couple hours. But, nope. That's not what happened.

The stool was encircled by a metal band which crushed his skull at the point of impact. His death was ruled a homicide by blunt force trauma.

I was sentenced to death.

Now, here I was. My life was being offered up to me on a silver platter. All I had to do was reach out and take it. Plus, whatever External Security was asking of me.

I can't lie. My stomach was full of butterflies, each flap of their silky wings causing tendrils of fear to spread throughout my core. Like my body knew that life only paid for life with life. What was my life worth? To me, it was priceless.

But, what was my life worth to the Nation of Elan and its External Service?

Nothing.

Or, at least I couldn't see where my value lay for the powers that be. At twenty-five years of age, I'd spent most of my adult life in this cell, so I wasn't particularly educated. I wasn't born into money and didn't have friends in high places. I didn't have any specialized skills, or some fundamental expertise.

I was just a man living his life, until I became a man awaiting his death.

But the truth was I wanted to live.

A variety of emotions rushed through me. Hope was mostly what I felt. I hadn't felt hope in what seemed an eternity. And, now that I was experiencing it... man, was it powerful. I could have what I'd thought was lost forever. I could let go of this mental clock hanging over my head, ticking, ticking, ever so slowly toward my execution. I could make plans. Planning for a future was an activity of which I'd had no need. Actually, it was downright depressing. I knew with absolute certainty that any plans would never have a chance to come to fruition.

How could I refuse?

"Ok," I said. "I'll do it."

"Great!" He clapped his hands together. "Follow me."

After sliding my feet into my sandals, I pulled a t-shirt over my head and followed Mays out of my cell. No handcuffs, no ankle chains. None of the security measures normally forced upon the condemned. We walked down the cell block hallway, passed doors behind which stood other condemned men who had been rousted from their sleep by the sounds of my door opening when no doors should be open, asking, "Where you going?"

Silently ignoring them all, we continued through the door into the hallway that connected this unit to the rest of the prison. After navigating our way to a garage used for picking up and dropping off prisoners, I was loaded into a black van.

The ride was short, maybe five minutes from one location to the other. Then I was hauled out into another garage, through another door, into another building. But, there was no comparison between the building I had just left and this place.

The carpet was so plush I could feel fibers tickling my toes, teasing me. I wanted to stop right there, slide my feet from my sandals, and dig my digits into the cloud-like caress of the carpet. The walls were free of grime and painted a bright white. Indistinguishable office doors flashed past as we hurried down the hallway. There were no numbers or labels on the doors.

No cells.

After a zig and a zag, I was ushered into one of the offices and left to myself the door clicked as it closed behind me. I looked around, although there wasn't much to look at. In the middle of the slightly-larger-than-my-cell sized room was a modernist style table and chair. On the table was a glass of water and a platter with meats, cheese, and crackers. Embedded in the wall across from the chair was a screen that came to life as I sat and picked up a piece of cheese, startling me.

Gerent Jefferson Malbent appeared on screen with the national seal behind him. "Gerent" is the term we use for our leader. Such as the American's President, before America as a nation ceased to exist.

He said, "As Gerent of Elan, I'd like to personally thank you for accepting this mission. It is extremely important to our nation and our citizens. As you're probably aware, Elan has little to no oil reserves and absolutely no oil production. In order for our nation to grow and unite this land as it once was, we need oil. Our neighbors to the south refuse to sell us any. Time and time again I've tried to bring Gutenberg to the negotiating table. The people of Elan *need* this resource, yet they deny us, as if we have nothing to offer in return."

He straightened his tie and cleared his throat before continuing. "That is about to change. This is why you're here."

His hands came into view from opposite sides of the screen, each holding a small vial. A blue cap topped the vial in his right hand, a yellow cap topped the left.

Thrusting the blue capped vial forward, he said, "This is a new virus based on the Z-20 strain. I'm sure you remember the wars and how bad it was until a treatment and vaccine were developed. Your job is to disperse this virus above Gutenberg."

The blue top disappeared from the screen, leaving the yellow topped vial, which he pushed toward the camera. "This is the antidote. Completely neutralizes the virus, and its effects are immediate. This gives us a bargaining chip, a reason for them to sit down at the table and negotiate a deal with us. This gives us a chance. You'll receive your orders and detailed mission plan shortly. Good travels, and may The One bless us with his favor."

2

JASON

The screen turned black and the door immediately opened. They'd either been standing right outside the door listening, or had received some signal letting them know the Gerent's speech was over. Agent Mays entered, followed by a dark-haired woman with oversized blue eyes.

Mays said, "Did you enjoy the platter? Hopefully, it lived up to your expectations?" His head dipped towards the barely touched food.

Our charismatic leader had consumed my attention to the extent that I'd forgotten about the full plate before me.

"Well," Mays said, "time to go. Shall we?"

At the risk of seeming uncouth, I grabbed a handful of meat, cheese, and crackers before trailing Agent Mays and the lady back into the hallway. We approached an elevator, its doors wide open. Entered. There were no buttons, no panel next to the door. Only a small, barely discernible camera in the back corner above our heads.

The doors closed as soon as we entered, and I felt the car begin to lower. Once it stopped, we stepped out into a laboratory. Unfamiliar smells assaulted my senses. Some reminiscent of burning rubber, layered on top of something astringent. Others were simply indescribable.

This was no biological lab. Not even close. A menagerie of gadgets and gizmos were strewn all over the place. Most were inanimate, but some were scurrying, or rolling, and even flying about the place. This was a robotics and engineering lab.

This was R&D.

There were even weapons. A variety of stun guns rested on tables, and some were even being tested, their prongs crackling with energy.

Mays said, "We'll be outfitting you with a delivery drone and you'll be able to choose a few weapons. You'll be traveling alone and once you're outside of the city things can be dangerous. Make your selections and let's be off."

The first thing I grabbed was a long knife and its sheath. This wouldn't be just a weapon. A good knife could be used for all kinds of stuff, from cutting branches off a tree to cutting up food. With a long journey ahead, I was sure the knife would see its fair share of use.

As I was browsing the tasers, I noticed one looked more like a gun, only it was a little clunkier. It had a magazine that released from the bottom of the grip. Small, flat cartridges with short prongs at one end filled the magazine. No wires connected cartridge to weapon.

"Like that?" a voice from behind said. "We call it the Scythe."

I turned around and came face to face with a man in a white lab coat and large, round glasses.

"The cartridges have a battery. Fire and forget. A selector on the side lets you switch from non-lethal to lethal. I've seen one of these bad boys take down a bull!"

Picking up the Scythe, I fingered the selector, flicking the switch up and down. Aimed it. Then I set it aside, along with the knife. The guy in the lab coat brought five extra magazines and put them next to the Scythe.

Firearms were a rare sighting in Elan. Almost all of the ammunition supply for the entire world had been used during the Z Wars. It had even reached a point where most people were defending themselves with either bladed or club style weapons. And, after, people were focused on rebuilding communities and society. I was sure some nation somewhere was producing ammo, but not here.

We *did* have an abundance of electricity, though.

Elan lay in a valley, between two mountain ranges, creating a natural wind corridor. Before the Z Wars, this valley was a hotspot for wind energy and battery technology. Our society was centered around electricity. As such, electricity powered our weapons.

Along with everything else.

A small handheld taser and an e-spear rounded out my selections. The lab tech took my items and disappeared toward the back.

Mays said, "He'll meet us on the way out with all of your things."

The next room we entered was full of various items of clothing. Rack after rack lined the room, creating neat, narrow aisles. An attendant approached me, his arms extending this way and that way, taking measurements and sizing me up. I wasn't a big guy. Average in size, average in height. It didn't take him long. Then, he led me to a rack where I tried on a few things.

He'd done a good job when he estimated my fit, so I went down the rack, picking out everything I thought I'd need, finishing with a dark, heavy cloak. After putting on the outfit I wanted to wear, the attendant took everything else to the back.

After leaving the closet - as I'd come to think of it - we made a return trip to the elevator, back through the maze of corridors, and into the garage. The van loomed before me, its side door gaping open in invitation.

"Your bags are already inside. Agent Reece will take it from here," Mays said, gesturing toward the dark haired woman. Then, he turned and went back into the building.

Reece nodded her head towards the open door, my signal to climb in. So, I did, taking my former seat. Gazing down, I noticed what looked to be two large backpacks connected to each other with a thick strap. A third bag, resembling a small, flat duffel rested next to the backpacks.

The van silently took off. Agent Reece still hadn't spoken. Not a single word. The quiet whine of the van's electric motor was the only thing to keep me company, but we pulled to a stop a short time later. Reece got out and opened my door, enabling my first view of the outdoors in five years.

The sun was rising, and I could see its glow casting a halo above the canopy of the surrounding trees. I walked around the van, bringing the rest of the area into my vision. Agent Reece took off walking past a large, white house with crimson shutters toward a stable that was to the right and slightly behind the house.

In the gap between house and stable I paused and looked out over acres of rolling meadow, the wooden outlines of corrals and horse pens breaking up the monotonous green.

A sharp whistle interrupted my thoughts, and when I looked around, Agent Reece was waving me into the stables.

As I crossed inside, Reece spoke for the first time, her voice soft and melodic, "You ride?"

"Been a while," I responded.

"Pick one."

Horses lined both sides, so I chose the right side and walked from horse to horse, spending a few moments with each. Once I reached the last horse, I crossed to the other side and did the same ritual until I'd made my way back to Reece. Then I went back down the right side, stopping at one particular mare that nuzzled her nose into the palm of my hand.

"This one," I said.

Reece opened the stall and bridled the horse. Handing me the reins, she went to a stall on the other side and bridled a horse of her own.

After leading our mounts out of the stables, she told me to grab the bags from the van. Once I'd returned, Agent Reece walked me through saddling up and securing the saddlebags to my horse.

Yeah, that's right. The backpacks were saddlebags.

Then she went to the front seat of the van and came back with a holster for the Scythe and a scabbard for the e-spear. After handing both to me, I put the holster on my hip and attached the scabbard to my horse, inserting the corresponding weapon as I did so.

"What's her name?" I asked as I mounted my horse.

"That's Pepper."

Gutenberg lay to the south, so we turned south once we reached the road. Pepper was easygoing and responded well. Agent Reece was obviously an experienced rider. And I was enjoying the hypnotic *clop, clop* of hooves as we made our way down the road, sprinkles of the morning sun shining through the canopy, guiding our way.

"You sure you're ok with what you're about to do?" Reece asked.

"To be honest, I'm not really thinking about it. Not yet, at least. I do know that I prefer living to dying, and if I have to prove that my life is worth living I'm going to do it."

We turned right, heading west, and then we rode in silence until we came upon the on-ramp for a highway that ran north to south.

"The drone is in your bag," she said. "Fly it to the middle of the city, then straight up to five-hundred feet. The canister will explode once it reaches altitude."

After pausing for a second, Reece said, "There's something different about you."

She turned her horse around, dug her heels into its side, and let out a short, *ya!*

Reece took off down the road at a trot.

Pepper and I climbed the on-ramp, heading south.

3

BRIT

Once upon a time, the inn had been part of a chain, with hundreds of locations spread out across America. Its rooms had seen the faces of thousands of travelers. Its breakfast buffet had filled the bellies of those travelers. But, that was before. Before the pandemic. Before the sickness. Before the dead.

Now, it was a stop on the road for the occasional weary men, and sometimes women, who journeyed along the highway between Elan and Gutenberg. It offered respite to the intermittent trader who went from community to community in search of goods. It was also a place where wandering outlaws could get a home cooked meal and a mug of beer or wine.

As Brit wiped the surface of the bar with a moist towel, candle light flickered in the gloomy room. Tendrils of smoke rose from the homemade candles, then disappeared into the darkness.

Two men whistled for her attention, then waved her over.

As she approached their table, a stench assaulted her nostrils, causing her stomach to tighten, but she continued on. Since the outbreak, bad smells had become a part of daily life.

The men looked as if they hadn't had a bath in a month. Their hair and beards were all matted and uncombed. Their clothes looked dusty, as if she'd create a sandstorm if she blew too hard in their direction.

"How may I help you?" she asked once she'd arrived.

"Oh, I can think of a few different ways," the guy on the right stated. Wearing dark boots and jeans that had seen better days, he lifted his hand to his face and stroked his ratty, blond beard.

Brit had grown accustomed to slick remarks from men. The truth was, she was attractive. To the point that she used to be embarrassed by it. And, after the world went crazy, her beauty had proven to be a curse at times.

So, she ignored him and steeled her voice as she repeated, "How may I help you?"

The other guy spoke up, his dark eyes consuming the dancing light as he said, "We'll take a couple beers. And whatever's cooking in the back."

She went back to the bar, calling their order to the cook. Opening the spout of the barrel sitting on top of the bar, she poured two cups, cutting the flow right as the head reached the top. Once she'd returned from delivering the beers, two bowls of a thick chicken and vegetable stew were waiting in the window.

Bowls in hand, Brit trekked back to their table.

"So... What's the price for a piece of you?" Dark Boots asked after she sat their bowls down.

Her hand shot out, and she slapped the man across his face, the sharp sound reverberating throughout the bar.

His chair toppled to the hardwood floor as he jerked to his feet and took a step towards Brit. The man with the dark eyes was right behind him, but he stretched an arm across Dark Boots' chest.

"Relax, friend, and eat. It's not often we get to enjoy such a hearty meal." Hanging in matted coils, his dark hair was a compliment to his dark eyes. His voice was deep and soft. He was tall.

Brit strained her neck as she looked up at him.

Dark Boots stroked his blond beard again, then grunted. He kicked his chair upright and sat back down.

Brit turned back to the bar, her heart racing. Old memories stabbed at her gut as she fought to keep them locked away, buried in the darkest corners of her mind. Memories that sometimes visited in her dreams, when she was vulnerable and couldn't beat them back into repression.

But, she was wide awake and rapidly got herself under control.

The two men soon left after causing no more trouble, then Brit went back to her daily chores.

The inn belonged to her aunt Michelle, her last known, surviving relative. After the wars, her aunt just moved into the place and started fixing it up. It was in the middle of nowhere, but next to what used to be a major highway, so Michelle figured it may attract a few travelers; with the benefit of its remote location, she just might be able to make it profitable.

Brit crossed into the kitchen, weaved around stainless steel workstations, most of which hadn't been used in forever, and went out of the back door. Standing next to a large dumpster, she looked out across the open land that she and her aunt had cleared to make space for a garden, grazing for a couple dairy cows, and horse stables for overnighters who traveled by mount.

The day was fast approaching sunset as she made her way to the stables. This was Brit's place of solace, her refuge. She even loved being out there when the occasional horse was there. But today, it was empty.

The first stall was basically a storage area with a stool in the corner. As she turned into it, the scrape of a shoe could be heard behind her.

Turning around to check out the noise, Brit was caught off guard as a hand clamped around her throat. She looked up and stared into a familiar, blond beard.

"Thought you were going to get away with putting your hands on me?" Dark Boots reared his head back and spit in her face. Then, he smiled.

The thick saliva oozed down her face, creating little streamlets that tickled as they flowed toward her chin.

"You're going to make a good, little bed warmer for someone," Dark Boots said.

Brit brought her leg up and kicked him in the groin. As he howled and dropped to his knees in pain, she ran around him and out of the entrance of the stables, running head first into the chest of the tall man with the dark eyes.

He wrapped his arms around Brit, pinning her arms to her body.

Those old memories began swimming to the surface as fear tightened her gut. Shivers spread throughout her body, small aftershocks betraying her anxiety. Brit couldn't breathe, as if someone was tightening a tourniquet, restricting the expansion of her chest.

She thrashed in the man's arms, a hot anger starting to take over. She'd vowed to never be a victim again, to never submit to that level of abuse, pain, and self-loathing.

Never. Again.

But, her efforts offered no reward.

The man with the dark eyes was just too big, too strong, too in-control. She exhausted herself, but it was his calm silence that made her stop moving. He was completely unaffected by her struggle.

Her hands were taken and pinned behind her. A slight burning sensation stung the flesh of her wrists as a rope was tightly wrapped around them.

Then, a finger lightly brushed the side of her neck beneath

her long, black hair. She could feel Dark Boots' breath on her ear as he said, "We're going to get a pretty penny for you!" Then, he gave a little chuckle.

Brit's stomach dropped and bile rose into the back of her throat.

The tall man released her from his bear hug, and she immediately took off at a sprint. She didn't make it far, though. After about ten feet a searing pain tore at her shoulders as her arms were wrenched behind her, against her forward momentum. Stumbling a couple steps backwards, she fell to the dirt in front of the stables.

Dark Boots had secured a length of rope to her wrist bindings, acting as a leash.

He said, "Shit, Cody! She's a wily one!" A smile appeared through his beard. "I like it when they have a little spunk."

"Come on," Cody said, his dark eyes turning toward the tree line. "We need to get her to the broker. Let's not linger."

Brit looked at the inn. Her aunt was inside, ill, hard of hearing, and probably sleeping. It was doubtful that she'd hear anything. There had only been the two customers, so no valiant patron would be coming to her rescue. But, the cook was inside.

"*HEEEELP! Luis!*" She screamed at the top of her lungs.

A blow landed on the back of her head, bringing stars into her vision.

Luis came running out of the door and skidded to a stop as he took in the scene before him.

Cody walked toward him, slow and steady, said, "You should turn around and go back inside."

"Brit? What's going on?" Luis asked.

"Man, you should really go back inside right now," Cody said, as he continued closing the distance.

"Brit?"

The knife whispered as it was pulled from its sheath. Cody thrust it upward into Luis' abdomen.

Luis made a choking noise as he fell to his knees, clutching his stomach. Then, he looked down at his hands and the blood seeping through his fingers. A tear fell from each eye.

"*Luis! Noooooo!*" Brit cried. "You bastard!"

Struggling against her restraints, she tried to get to Luis. The ropes dug into her wrists, but he was dying right in front of her. Her shoulders screamed as they were yanked behind her, but his life force was spilling into the dirt.

Brit fell to her knees, hung her head. "Why?" she asked. "Why are you doing this?"

"Get up," Dark Boots said. "Time to go."

She couldn't get up, couldn't leave Luis. Not like this. Couldn't let him just die out here by himself.

Impatient, Dark Boots began dragging her. She fell over onto her side, the dirt and gravel scraping at her skin.

"Okay, okay. I'll walk."

He stopped, allowing her to stand.

As soon as she was on her feet the rope was tugged and she stumbled behind Dark Boots, into the tree line, closely followed by Cody.

4

THE GERENT

As the small group of men filed into the conference room, Gerent Malbent sat at the head of the enormous, mahogany table, silently watching as everyone took their seats. These men held key positions in Elan's political structure, and they also possessed massive wealth. They were the oligarchy, so to speak. Men with power and influence, overlords in their own right. Men who had taken the end of the world and turned it into the beginnings of their financial empires.

Last through the door was Vicar, The One's representative in the flesh. Flowing, white robes cloaked a thin frame, and a white head-piece rested on top of long, graying hair. His presence filled the room as he took a seat to the right of the Gerent.

"I've authorized an attack on Gutenberg," Gerent Malbent said as soon as Vicar was seated. "The first phase is already underway."

He stared at McClendon, who held the position of Minister of Treasury, and said, "Make sure The Colonel has whatever necessary to prepare the troops. Whatever the expense. This campaign must be successful. Am I understood?"

McClendon nodded his head and said, "Understood, Gerent."

Malbent shifted his gaze toward The Colonel. No one knew if he'd really been a Colonel before the pandemic, and if you got to know him you'd be doubtful. Sure, he could fight, he could strategize, and he had that often elusive quality of command. But, He could border on the sadistic, and had a lust for blood. Perfect to lead an army in this new world, but the old world had been too innocent. They had frowned upon water-boarding, and that's just an appetizer for anyone under interrogation by The Colonel.

"We march in two weeks, Colonel. Have the men ready."

"Sir," The Colonel said. "You said the first phase was already under way. May I ask exactly what that is?"

Malbent rose from his seat, catching the eye of Vicar, who issued a slight nod.

"We're deploying a modified version of the Z-20 virus inside of Gutenberg. That should soften those pompous pricks right up." He paced down the length of the table. "Once the chaos begins, we'll attack."

"Sir. I must advise against this course of action. Z-20 was extremely contagious and we're lucky to have survived it the first time. We can't let that cat out of the bag again," Ben Opoku, Minister of Internal Security, said.

"Why wasn't I told about this plan?" The Colonel boomed. "We could have coordinated and been better prepared. Did you know about this, Dean?"

Dean Wilson, Minister of External Security, was The Colonel's boss. Of a sort. Technically, the armed forces fell under External Security's purview, and The Colonel had always made it obvious that he didn't appreciate that fact. Even to the extent that he'd petitioned the Gerent to separate the two entities. But, Dean was smart, and had the ability to see into the future. Not to mention, he was as clever as a fox.

Dean nodded, and in his quiet voice said, "Yes."

"We can't do this," Ben repeated, his voice a little louder this time. "Innocent people will die. There must be another way!"

All eyes turned in Vicar's direction as he cleared his throat.

"The One has given this mission His blessing," Vicar said, his voice deep and steady. "We are righteous. We will reunite this land in the name of The One. Then, we will unify the world, so that all mankind may bask in His glory."

"The decision to conduct this strike has been made, and is final," Gerent Malbent said. "I will hear nothing more of it. Follow your orders and make this campaign successful. The lives lost will be remembered as martyrs and celebrated as heroes. Let's make sure their sacrifice has value."

Malbent stared into the eyes of each man, then dismissed them.

Vicar remained seated as everyone took their leave. As soon as the conference room had been emptied, he stood, and said to the Gerent, "Come with me. We have much to do."

Outside of the conference room, two guards fell into step slightly behind, and to either side of the Gerent, their red cloaks billowing behind them, contrasting against their pristine, white uniforms. Six guards in total formed the Gerent's protection detail, offering twenty-four-hour security. If they weren't standing slightly behind and beside the leader of Elan, they were right outside the door, ready to jump into action at the slightest threat to the Gerent.

Vicar led Malbent through the hallways of the industrial era factory, which had been remodeled into the Gerent's palace and offices. The two men took the elevator down the five level building, into the basement. After entering the spacious boiler room, they weaved around the skeletal remains of long forgotten mechanical equipment and stopped in front of a large piece of rusted steel that was shaped like a school bus, with a tangle of disconnected pipes that reminded Malbent of the tentacles of a schizophrenic squid. Vicar adjusted a small lever then pushed the hulking, steel machinery with surprising ease, revealing a hidden stairway beneath.

The faint glow of tiny LED lights illuminated the staircase as they made their descent into the bedrock. By the time they'd reached the bottom, the air had become heavy, oppressive even. Malbent felt the fingers of claustrophobia beginning to claw their way into his chest, squeezing at his lungs and heart. He reminded himself to breathe, to stay calm. Keep walking. He'd made this walk to Vicar's chambers a hundred times. He had this same reaction every single time. The Gerent had never been prone to claustrophobia. Never. He'd always thought that this response had more to do with Vicar himself and not the passageway.

After climbing another set of stairs at the other end of the tunnel, they emerged into a gloomy room. A small altar with thirty candles provided the only light, drawing your full attention to a black orb, its glowing green veins pulsing in the flickering candle light as it rested in the position of honor on top of the altar.

Vicar knelt before the altar, head raised as if he were basking in the sun on a bright spring day and sat there silently, unmoving. No rise and fall of his chest as he inhaled, then exhaled. Nothing.

The Gerent wondered if Vicar was still living. But, no. Men like Vicar don't die easily.

"Send delegates to Eastshore and Highland," Vicar said as he floated to his feet. "Tell them that the virus has made a resurgence and we're the only nation with a vaccine and cure. In exchange for access to our medicines, they will support our camping against Gutenberg and give us a thousand men for the fight. Send the delegates immediately, for the day fast approaches that we march on Gutenberg."

"And if they refuse?" Malbent asked.

"They'll be signing their own death warrants. The virus will reach them one way or another. Make it clear that if they don't join us now, then they can't come asking for our help once their citizens begin ripping each other to pieces. Those who do not support the will of The One shall receive no mercy."

Vicar led Malbent and the two guards up a flight of stairs, to the temple above.

He said, "Ben is going to be a problem. Think I'll have a visit with him."

The Gerent responded, "No, he won't. I've known him since the wars. He may voice his opinion whenever we're in council, but he'll fall in line."

As they emerged into Vicar's office proper, at the back of the temple, he said, "Well, he's your friend, your responsibility. By the love of The One, don't make me have to intervene."

Vicar sat at a desk made of dark, tightly grained wood. Behind him was another orb, this one much larger than the other, but its green veins didn't pulse and lacked the energy you could feel downstairs. Still, it made for an impressive sight.

Before Vicar could begin speaking again, the sharp rap of knuckles on wood interrupted the silence. He gave the Gerent a nod and, turning toward the guard standing before the front office door, Malbent issued a nod of his own.

The guard opened the door, revealing a Priest of the Highest, who was obviously startled by the sight of the e-spear crackling to life, its foot-long, brightly glowing arc blocking the entrance. After a few menacing seconds the guard allowed the priest to enter, his black robe flowing as he rushed into the room.

Gerent Malbent was appreciative of the interruption and used it as an excuse to take his leave.

5

———

JASON

The city had once been full of life. You couldn't tell by looking at it now, but the mid-sized city had once held a few hundred thousand people. That was before. Before the wars. Before it had become a pile of rubble. Before the guns, and the mortars, and the bombs.

At least it was still here. Hundreds of years from now, archaeologists will comb through the ruins in an effort to chronicle the events that had taken place. The same can't be said of the larger cities.

Pepper clop-clopped along the cracked pavement at an easy pace as I looked around. Mother Nature wasted no time reclaiming what had belonged to her. Tall weeds sprang up from the sidewalk, determined, refusing to be denied the embrace of the warm sun. Tree branches pierced the slanted roofs of homes as broken windows bared their jagged teeth at the world. Vines and moss crept over the facades as if slowly binding the structures, preventing them from escaping Mother's restoration efforts.

It suddenly dawned on me how much effort people put into keeping Her at bay. Without our intervention, nature

30

flourishes. We obviously need Her much more than She needs us.

Pepper and I skirted around the city, avoiding potential bandits. The crumbling buildings were capable of providing some shelter, but that was about it. You couldn't farm, raise livestock, or do pretty much anything necessary for self-sustained living in these times.

Just hide out after robbing someone who happened to be traveling along the highway.

Circling the city had taken the majority of an uneventful afternoon, but the sun was getting low and I needed to find a place to bed down for the night. A river flowed north to south through the city, and I met it just south of the city, following its meandering current into the suburbs. As the ghosts of houses past slowly gave way to larger swaths of green countryside, I kept my eyes peeled for suitable shelter.

An old mill floated into view. As I approached, the signs of Mother Nature's reclamation efforts were apparent, but the mill lacked the man-made destruction seen in the city. The doors and windows were missing, exposing the interior to the elements, but the stone structure looked sound.

Pepper grazed as I filled a container with water. Then, I gathered a few pieces of old wood and started a fire.

An old lullaby my mother would sing came to mind, and I sang the tune softly. This had become my habit while I'd been on death row. Didn't even know that I had remembered the song, but one day the words and melody sprang into my mind, riding the gentle waves of my mom's voice as I sat on the floor of my cell, despair weighing heavily on my shoulders as I thought about how I'd landed myself on the row. Her words had been the comforting caress that I'd needed, and I kept that song on my breath daily.

And, today, just as that day, I thought about the opening scene to this particular act in my life.

THE CANNABAR WAS PACKED, colorful LEDs bathing the crowd of people in a kaleidoscope of blues, reds, and greens. Tendrils of smoke lazily floated through the vibrant atmosphere, as some people writhed to the pounding beat of the music that was blaring from the oversized speakers. Others were seated, either at the bar or in a booth, smoking, drinking, and laughing.

The woman had been sitting at the bar when a man approached and bought her a drink, inviting her back to the table where he'd been sitting with two other guys.

After accepting the invite, she joined the guys at the table, where things soon started to get uncomfortable for her.

Cannabars were fertile grounds for women in the pleasure industry. Hordes of men came to drink, get high, and toss their valuables and silver at anything with a pretty face willing to offer them a night of pleasure in return.

But, this woman had never before seen the inside of a pleasure house. She was completely out of her league in this place. Or, maybe, she was out of the cannabar's league.

She was beautiful, true. Wild, curly hair framed big, dark eyes. But, she carried herself with a certain air. Walking with her head held high, she floated across the room with the confidence of a lion and the grace of a ballerina.

I was coming from the bathroom, and, turning the corner out of the hallway, I bumped right into her.

"I'm sorry," I said. "Excuse me."

After taking a step past me, she turned around, and said, "I need some air. Wanna walk outside with me?"

"Um... Sure," I responded.

We were just beyond the bar, heading toward the door when the three men she'd been sitting with approached us.

I'd seen her sitting with the trio before going to the bathroom, so as they walked up, I just looked on to see how it would play out.

"Where do you think you're going?" one of the guys asked. "You're with us for the night."

After that panty dropping pick-up line, he took hold of her slim wrist with a blue collar hand.

Snatching her arm from his grip, she said, "No."

Not loud. Not in an effort to raise alarm. Just loud enough for our small group to hear and know she meant it.

Furious, the guy took a step in her direction.

My hand made contact with his chest, halting his progress. After looking down at my offending hand, he met my eye.

"She said, no." My voice was steel.

He took a swing, that blue collar hand flying in a wide arc toward my face. I saw it late, and the fist blew past me so close I could feel the wind upon my cheek as I turned my head away from the punch at the last possible second.

I unleashed a flurry of lefts and rights, the onslaught too much for him to handle, and he fell to the bar's floor. Every set of eyes in the building turned toward the disturbance.

Something crashed onto my back, between my shoulder blades, sending tingles of pain down my spine. Turning around just as the second swing was winding up, I ducked my head down low and rushed him as the chair arced over me. He crashed backward, into the bar, his left arm knocking a few drinks off. My left forearm went to his throat as I hit him in the stomach with a heavy blow. A grunt escaped his lips, and he began throwing weak punches at my face as he twisted his head side to side in an effort to relieve the pressure on his neck.

A dull pain thudded in my jaw, and the world flashed brightly for a second as I stumbled to the side. The third guy had hit me with one hell of a punch. My bell rang for a moment as I tried to get my bearings. Then, another punch slammed into my nose.

Eyes watering, I blindly reached out for something, anything to hold on to. The wind was knocked from my lungs as a fist buried itself in my stomach, followed by a strike to my ribs. Right on top of my liver. My knees went weak, and I fell to the floor.

Crawling away from the beating, my hand bumped into something. I grabbed it.

The leg of a bar stool.

Using it to support my weight, I climbed back to my feet. I saw movement out of the corner of my eye as my better-than-I-was opponent moved in. I spun, the leg of the bar stool still in my hand. Everything I had left in me went into the movement. I didn't even feel it connect. The only thing I felt was pain. My body was throbbing. My face was throbbing. My lungs were burning as they gasped for breath after breath.

But, I heard it. The sound was like a pecan being crushed by a nutcracker, amplified a hundred times.

The man fell to the floor. The stool fell to the floor. I looked around. The girl was gone.

Most everybody was gone.

Taking baby steps toward the door as bolts of pain flashed through my body, I slowly made my way out of the cannabar and into the parking lot. Where I ran right into three IS officers.

"Internal Security!" one of the men screamed. "Get down on the ground now!"

If I'd gotten on the ground, I may have never gotten up.

The bar's patrons had all filed into the lot outside, and as I searched the crowd of faces, I kept my eyes peeled for one in particular.

Didn't see her.

But, I felt a thump as something hit my chest. Looking down, I saw a small cartridge clinging to me, its prongs buried just beneath my skin. Then, I felt a jolt as the electricity started flowing. Everything went weak.

Then, everything went black.

6

BRIT

"Get up! Get up!" the man screamed, waking her from a very uncomfortable sleep. There was a shackle around her neck, making for a very cumbersome collar, and finding a position that didn't make her feel like she was about to choke to death had been next to impossible.

After removing a key from his pocket, Dark Boots unlocked and unwrapped from around a large oak the chain connecting her collar to those of nine others. After slinging the chain over his shoulder, he took off walking at a fast pace, tugging them behind.

"Get a move on! We must reach the broker by night tomorrow and we have many miles to cover," he said, giving the chain a yank. "If we don't make it I'll have all your hearts for dinner, you can count on that. Now, move!"

Groggy from lack of rest, the prisoners stumbled along, out of the woods, onto a weathered two lane road.

Dark Boots in the front, Cody at the rear.

After about an hour, Brit, tired of tasting the dry, gritty taste in her mouth, said, "I need water. We need water. Nobody will reach the broker if we all die of thirst."

Cody responded, "No one will die of thirst. Keep walking. You'll get a drink soon enough."

The guy directly behind Brit in their chain gang whispered in a voice that only she could hear, "Thanks."

She turned her head just enough to see him. With bronze skin, long, black hair, and a face devoid of any facial hair, Brit put him at about eighteen.

Offering a slight nod in response, she focused on the road ahead and trudged onward.

Left untamed, foliage crept right up to the street, threatening to overrun the road. Up ahead, the burnt-out remnants of an old car rested at a forty-five degree angle in the middle of the street. The problem with traveling long distances by vehicle was that there were so many roadblocks. Cars were stalled out, tree branches stretched across roads, obstacles of all kinds made it almost impossible to travel long distances without a caravan of workers dedicated to clearing the roads along the way. Not to mention the lack of refueling options. So, most people traveled long distances by horseback.

Or, they walked.

Approaching what would have once been called a bridge, its center now missing, crumbled into the stream below, Dark Boots led the group down an embankment to the gently flowing water of the stream.

"See? Water," Dark Boots said. "Nobody died. Drink your fill, then let's be off."

The ten prisoners dropped to their knees in unison, as the chain linking their collars prevented them from moving individually, and drank. Brit splashed water on her face, wiping away the grime of the past couple days. The water was cool, refreshing, and even this small bit of a wash-up did wonders for Brit's morale.

"I'm Sanjay." The guy who'd been walking behind her, but

was now squatting beside her, introduced himself. "What's your name?"

"Brit."

"You're pretty," Sanjay said.

"We're on our way to be sold as slaves, and you find this to be the perfect time to hit on me?"

"I was just saying..." He stammered as he spoke. "I'm sorry."

"It's ok," she smiled. "How long have you been with these guys?"

"They caught me two days before you came. I'm from the coast. Was out collecting mussels at low tide, then all of a sudden these two guys were standing over me."

"They took me from my aunt's inn. There's ten of us and two of them. Surely, we can take them," Brit suggested.

The chain linking their collars was yanked, causing a pain up her neck as the prisoners were all pulled over onto their sides.

"Get up! Time to go!" Dark Boots' voice grinded her eardrums.

They followed the stream for a while, then veered onto a game trail. Brit thought she heard a wolf howling in the distance, but wasn't sure. She'd only known wolves to be creatures of the night. To hear one in the middle of the day was odd.

Sanjay finally spoke, "There was a guy. Tried to get the jump on the big, dark haired one-"

"Cody," she interrupted.

"Yeah, him."

"So, what happened?" she asked.

"They... They beat him. Then, the blond one..." His bronze skin took on a reddish tint.

"What? Tell me," Brit said, maybe a little too passionately.

"He. He, shoved-"

"Quit yer yapping back there!" Dark Boots boomed.

"What?" Brit asked Sanjay. "Tell me."

Sanjay hung his head.

The pain in her side was sharp and came from nowhere. Brit spun her head just as the second blow was about to land.

"Didn't I tell you to shut it!" Dark Boots stood next to her, a weathered, hardwood flog in his hand.

The second blow made her knees weak, but as she was about to fall, the metal edge of her collar dug into her neck, and she kept her footing.

"It's going to be fun breaking you! Too bad I won't be there to see it. You're probably going out to the Western Badlands."

"And, you're going to die," Brit whispered, under her breath.

But Dark Boots heard, and gave her a couple more strikes from the flog.

After Dark Boots went back to the front of the line and their convoy took off again, Sanjay reached forward and gave her hand a squeeze.

She thought about her ailing aunt. The last time Brit had been taken by two sexually deviant brothers, back during the Z Wars, her aunt had formed a team to track her down, Brit's captors receiving justice in the process. But, not this time. Her aunt had been tough and strong back then. Born during the Laotian Civil War, she traveled to America as a refugee at the age of ten. She'd been fighting her entire life.

But, not now. There would be no rescue. No tough old broad kicking in the door with a hatchet clutched in her hand.

And, Luis...

The trail opened up to a small clearing, and as they crossed, Brit noticed a couple saddle bags sitting off to the side, along the edge of the clearing.

She wasn't the only one.

"Cody," Dark Boots said, as he pointed toward the bags. "See that over there?"

Cody merely grunted.

"Wonder if there's any coin?"

"Surely, no one would leave a bag full of silver lying around," Cody replied. "But grab it and let's keep moving. We'll be making camp soon."

After running over to the bags, Dark Boots slung the bags over his non-chain carrying shoulder then ran back and got the human train going again.

7

JASON

The morning air was crisp and clear as I got Pepper saddled up. Sleep had been uneasy, I still hadn't adjusted to not sleeping behind a locked door with only the sound of recycled air to accompany me. The woods, the world, was alive. The night was filled with all manner of chirps, songs, clicks, and calls. The sudden vibrancy of the night had awakened ancient nighttime fears, preventing sleep.

Sleeping behind a locked door did inspire a fair amount of safety.

Once I got Pepper put together, we followed the river for a while, but it cut into a small canyon and we had to travel a game trail that took a different direction, although still heading south.

A light breeze blew, carrying with it the scent of composting plant matter with a slight undertone of some sweet flower. Pleasant enough, and by mid-afternoon I started hearing the faint sound of water nearby.

The trail opened up to a meadow, and I figured this would be a good time to get some water and have a bite to eat. After relieving Pepper of her load, keeping only the e-spear, I led her toward the sound of water and soon came upon a stream.

Pepper drank. I drank, filled my bottle, and drank some more. Then I washed up, sweat and dust floating away down the stream.

Done, we started walking back to the meadow so she could graze and I could eat, the return trip seemingly quicker. As the meadow spread out before us, I searched the ground, looking for my bags.

I'd left them *right there.*

I shook my head and blinked a few times as if I were trying to wake myself from a dream. But, I knew.

Someone had taken my bags.

Fuck!

Someone had just stolen the beginning of the next apocalypse. All they had to do was fly it to five-hundred feet. And, nobody would have a clue.

I had to get that drone back before some unwitting fool began playing with what he didn't understand.

Searching around for disturbances to indicate which way they'd gone, I noticed a game trail that seemed as if a large band had come trampling through. Should be easy enough to track, but I wasn't sure I could take on such a large contingent.

Still, I followed their trail on foot, Pepper's reins in hand as she clopped beside me.

As the sun began its descent into the far horizon, their camp came into view. After taking Pepper and tying her up a couple hundred yards back, I crept through the dense foliage to the camp.

Two men were building a fire. One tall and dark of hair, the other shorter and fair. But what really struck me was the ten people sitting on the ground, side by side, all linked together by a chain around their necks, the end of which was wrapped around a tree.

Slavers.

And on the far side of their fire building efforts: my bags.

One of the slaves, a girl with long, dark hair and high cheekbones, turned around. She turned toward me and met my eye.

The world shook. Or, at least it did for me. The pull was so strong that I was afraid I'd walk out of the brush and reveal myself. It was a thirst, more powerful than a yearning. Tugging at my chest, wanting to pull me into her immediate presence.

Finally breaking eye contact, she offered a small shake of her head, then turned back toward the growing fire.

What was that! Never had I experienced a feeling like that when looking at a woman. Or anyone. Starting to feel like it had all been imagined, I began doubting what I'd just felt. Never a believer in love at first sight, this was more like the attraction between two strong magnets. Less an appeal of the heart and more a molecular gravitation. Like my entire being was just drawn to her.

A shiver ran through me.

I was relieved that she'd turned back around.

Once the sun had set, I crept around to where the two guys sat on a log. I removed the Scythe from its holster. After lining up my first shot, I squeezed the trigger.

The cartridge released with a quiet puff of air, sailed through the air, and lodged itself into the back of the blond guy. As the electrical charge dispersed, he tensed up, the muscles and tendons of his neck straining to the point where I thought they would snap, and fell over on the log. He slid to the earth.

As soon as the cartridge struck his friend, the dark haired guy dropped to the ground, and my second shot sailed over his head.

I sat there for a minute, waiting, but he didn't raise his head again, and there was no way I'd get another shot with that log in my way.

After re-holstering the Scythe, I rose to my feet, e-spear in hand, and brought it to life. The foot-long arc crackled and hissed, its bright, bluish glow illuminating the night.

Charging the log, I ran all out, then thrust the e-spear down when I saw the man lying on the ground, blade in hand. He rolled away from the arc, and up onto a knee. Stood to his full height.

The blade in his hand was a machete, sharp and efficient. Swinging it in a figure eight, he was comfortable with his weapon.

Raising the e-spear to block his first attack, I caught the machete with the spear's steel shaft. The rubber coated hand grips dampening the shock of steel colliding with steel. A kick to the stomach made me take a couple steps backward, and I stumbled over the log.

Rolling to my feet as he charged, I dove to the side, then regained my footing.

I thrust the spear toward him, and in an attempt to parry the thrust, the blade of his machete made contact with the arc of the e-spear. Jumping back, he immediately dropped the conductive steel blade.

After looking around for a brief second, he dove toward his unconscious friend and came up with an old wooden flog in hand.

He swung low at my legs. Hopping out of range a little too slowly, I got clipped on the calf, and, *did it hurt*. But I didn't have time to think about it because his next swing was coming in high, and I'd be damned if I let him hit me in the head with that thing.

My spear's shaft caught his flog, and after parrying the glorified stick to the side, I hit him in the nose with the butt of the spear.

After taking a step back, he made to block my next swing, the wood making contact with the glowing arc. Only this time no current flowed through the insulating wood. The arc *did* cut through the flog like a hot knife to butter.

In a desperate move, he threw the rest of the stick and ran at me full speed.

Dropping to a knee and evading his projectile, I stood back to my feet, e-spear ahead, piercing his chest. As the scent of burning flesh reached my nose, I immediately killed the e-spear, and the man fell to the ground. Dead.

Needing to catch my breath, I rested my hands on my knees for a minute. Then, I went to my bags.

"Hey! You're not going to leave us, are you? Set us free. They were going to sell us into slavery! Please," a man pleaded.

I wasn't planning on leaving them chained to a tree. I just wanted to make sure the drone hadn't been messed with.

It wasn't.

After slinging my bags over my shoulder, I walked over to the ten prisoners, picking up the machete on the way. I could have found the key on one of those guys, I was certain, but the adrenaline was still flowing through me and chopping a tree down with a machete seemed like a good way to push it through my system.

So, I hacked, and hacked, and hacked at the tree, and it fell sooner than I'd expected. The machete was sharp, though.

I'd be keeping it.

Yet to make eye contact with the girl again, I tried to leave the camp and keep it that way, but that wasn't to be.

"You felt it, didn't you?" she asked as she approached from behind.

8

———

JASON

Of course I'd felt it. Never felt anything as powerful. I just didn't know what it was. And I definitely didn't know what to do about it.

"What was that?" she asked.

Shrugging my shoulders, I said, "Whatever it was could have gotten me killed."

"But, why? I've never felt anything like that before. What does it mean?" She was following me.

"I don't know," I said, frustrated, and turned around.

It happened again. Not as powerful this time around, but it was still significant.

Feeling that inexorable pull, we moved closer, and I couldn't stop myself. When we were face to face she put a hand on my chest, stopping me, stronger than I.

Lifting my hand to her face, we made contact skin to skin. My entire body hummed with an energy that coursed through my veins; my skin tingled, my heart beat kicked into overdrive.

She felt it, too. It was written all over her face as I stared into her dark eyes.

Breaking contact, but still holding her eye, I felt that

magnetism significantly diminish. It was still there, though, buzzing right beneath the surface.

Turning around, I took off walking.

"Hey! Where are you going?"

"To get my horse," I responded.

"Who are you? What's your name?"

Facing her again, I felt that slight magnetism resume.

"I'm Jason."

"Brit. I'm Brit."

After retrieving Pepper, I rode back into the camp and noticed that only three of the ten remained. Brit, and two guys. They must have searched the guys and found the keys because their iron collars were conspicuously missing.

The two guys introduced themselves as Sanjay and Tristan.

"This is as good as any place to camp for the night. You can leave or stay. Your choice. I'm not really a fan of keeping people against their will. But if you decide to stay, I have food. And there's a fire," I said. "Mind helping me tie him up, though?" I gestured at the man on the ground.

"I have a better idea," Tristan said, holding one of the collars.

Still unconscious from the Scythe's cartridge, he offered a low groan as we hauled him to a tree and secured him.

I probed around in one of my bags and came out with a block of hard cheese, a small loaf of bread, and a dehydrated meal. Splitting everything equally, we ate in mostly silence. The only noise were the sounds of the night and the smacking of lips as Brit, Sanjay, and Tristan tore into their food.

After eating, everyone began talking, freedom and a little food washing away the tension of their previous situation and loosening their tongues. Brit was taken from an inn, Sanjay was from the coastal lands, and Tristan was from a community to the south, not far from where we were.

Me, on my way to Gutenberg.

"I'm heading south," I said to Tristan. "If you want to set out with me in the morning, you're more than welcome to."

"I'm coming, too," Brit said.

Tristan replied, "We have plenty of room." Turning to me, he said, "You could even stay, too. If you want."

"No. I mean, I'm going with Jason," Brit clarified.

"You can't," I said, feeling that ever present pull.

Wasn't sure I could get used to it.

"Why not?" she countered.

"Because..." I couldn't just tell her that I was on a mission to rain down an apocalypse upon a city full of people.

Raising an eyebrow, she stared a question at me that I couldn't answer.

"It's settled, then. I'm coming."

Unable to come up with a proper response, I let it rest. For now.

A chill came with the night, so I curled up beneath my cloak and soon fell asleep.

I was awakened by someone's sudden screams.

"Get back! Get back!" It was Sanjay.

Pepper was making all kinds of noise, snorting, neighing, and stamping her hooves.

Tristan, Brit, and I rose to our feet, simultaneously eyeing the wolf that was facing off with Sanjay, its teeth bared, body coiled like a spring, ready to attack.

From my experience, wolves travel in packs. To see a lone wolf was rare, indeed. To see a lone wolf attack a *group* of people was unheard of.

Spreading out beside Sanjay, we wanted to make our profile as large as possible, hoping that the wolf will understand it's outnumbered by a larger opponent and didn't stand a chance of winning this fight.

But the wolf just stood before Sanjay, teeth bared, ready to attack. Then five more wolves silently appeared from the darkness, their eyes glowing, reflecting the light of our dying fire.

Moving up, the wolves took positions next to their alpha.

This was bad.

Inching forward, the alpha looked like a real badass. Old scars lined his head and muzzle as a low rumble escaped his throat.

I can't lie. I was scared. Never before had I been surrounded by a pack of wolves. In my haste I'd left the e-spear on the ground, but the Scythe was on my hip. Not that it would do much good. I'd be able to get off one shot before the other wolves were on top of me.

The rest of the pack moved forward in anticipation of their alpha's move.

That energy buzzed through my body, again at its full intensity, and as it subsided, so too did the alpha's aggression. Lowering his tail between his legs, he arched his back as a whining sound came from his open mouth.

A chain reaction flowed through the rest of the pack as they, too, calmed down.

Then, the alpha turned and trotted away, the rest of the pack following his lead.

9

JASON

Upon waking the next morning, we immediately headed south toward Tristan's community, Holbrook. The morning was clear and fresh, dew coated the grass, birds were singing, and I took joy in it.

About an hour into our travels, Tristan blurted out, "What the hell was that last night, Jason?"

"What are you talking about?" I asked.

"You're joking, right?"

"A lot happened last night," I replied.

"What you did, with the wolves..."

A confused look was my response.

"You really don't know? Your eyes... They were, like, glowing. And it was like the air around you... You could *see* it," Tristan said.

Looking at Brit, I felt that pull becoming ever more familiar.

Nodding her head, she said, "Seriously. It was weird, but cool at the same time. Like you were a Super Saiyan, or something."

What!?

I was lost, my mind blank. They had to be messing with me.

That's not even possible. What they were telling me just didn't make sense. I'm sure I'd have known if my eyes were glowing.

Then, I remembered the buzz flowing through my body, and how the alpha had responded.

But how? That's impossible!

I didn't know what to say, so I silently walked alongside Pepper for most of the day. Worry had wedged itself in my mind. I didn't know what was happening to me. From what I'd felt when I looked into Brit's eyes, to them telling me that *my* eyes were glowing... And I didn't know what to make of what they'd said about the air around me. What would you even call it? A shimmer?

After stopping for a mid-afternoon lunch, we arrived at Holbrook as the sun was setting. A corrugated metal wall surrounded the small community. Probably a holdover from the Z Wars, constructed to keep the dead out and maintained after to ward off bandits. Bands of violent men and women were a constant threat to the small communities scattered throughout the badlands between the larger city-states with armies and internal security protocols. So, almost every community had them.

A man on top of the wall above the gate called down to his comrades, "Tangos approaching!" Then, after a minute, he said, "It's Tristan. Open the gate!"

After crossing through the gate we walked to the center of the community, first stopping at the community stables to put Pepper up for the night. The homes were of the cookie cutter variety popular right before the Z Wars, and land had been cleared around the outskirts of the neighborhood for agricultural purposes.

The main street was packed, the people in the midst of some festival or celebration. There were probably a couple hundred masked faces dancing, jumping, writhing, and chanting to the rhythmic beat of a drum. A fire pit with a goat skewered above the open flame sat at the end of the street, cradled in the curve of a cul-de-sac, filling the air with a savory scent that made my mouth water and brought about a rumble to my stomach.

Walking through the crowd, I noticed that all of the masks were animal themed. There were birds of every variety, wolves, bears, and tigers. Catching a whiff of another scent, I was reminded of the cannabars of my youth.

Tapping me on the shoulder, Tristan said, "Come with me."

After leading me to a house on the next street, he entered and called out, "Nana!"

An older woman with dreadlocks pulled into a ponytail shuffled into the front room, and upon seeing Tristan, her eyes lit up and she rushed over to give him a hug.

To her, Tristan said, "I was taken by a couple of slavers, but this guy saved us. His name is Jason."

Touching his face, she asked, "Are you alright?"

"Yes, Nana, I'm fine. A little hungry, that's all."

"Tell you what," she said. "I'll make some of my special jollof rice since we'll be hosting a hero."

"Thank you," I said.

An odd look crossed her face as she stared at me.

Tristan asked, "You speak Yoruba?"

"Yoruba?" That was a random question. "No. I don't."

"You spoke as if you understood her."

"I did. She was speaking plain English."

"No. She wasn't." Then, facing her, Tristan told the story of our encounter with the wolves the previous night.

When he finished, Nana told me to follow her to a room in the back that was more an apothecary than anything else. Taking a mortar and pestle, she ground a variety of herbs, dumping them into a silver bowl when she finished. After walking around the room gathering a few more ingredients, she tossed them in, as well.

Then, Nana lit a match and threw it into the bowl.

A green flame leapt out, but oddly, there was no heat.

"What do you know of the things Tristan described?" she asked me.

"That they're impossible."

"The future may only be unveiled as it happens, but the past has been written." She gave me a knife. "Cut your hand above the fire."

I did so, allowing my blood to drip, drip, drip into the green flame, which flared, then settled.

Inching her face closer to the fire, Nana stared raptly into its flickering green glow. She sat that way for minutes, which my impatient mind perceived as hours. I was thankful there wasn't a clock nearby, ticking away, forcing me to count every grueling second.

Finally, the fire died and she looked up.

"Interesting," she said.

"What is it?"

"Angels once walked the earth," she began.

ANGELS ONCE WALKED THE EARTH, finding the daughters of man beautiful, and took them as wives. Children were born of these unions. Giants, men of incredible strength, speed, and fighting ability. Men with powers.

These men were labeled monsters, abominations, and were to be destroyed by a flood. But a few escaped into Africa, where they built kingdoms, their progeny ruling for thousands of years.

Mbutu was one such kingdom, having rested at the foot of a mountain for nearly a thousand years. A prosperous kingdom, Mbutu had a wealth of gold, diamonds, and fertile agricultural lands.

Prosperity inspired envy from other kingdoms, resulting in numerous attacks that the armies of Mbutu successfully defended, campaigns led by Mbutu's powerful, majestic kings.

The Second World War brought about a different kind of invader in the German Nazis. Ahnenerbe - an organization helmed by Heinrich Himmler, who's true mission was to prove that the Aryan race were descendants of an advanced race of Nephilim, half men who'd been sired by Angels - had been recently incorporated into the 3rd Reich.

After receiving reports of the feats involving Mbutu's monarchy, the Reich dispatched a special detachment to track down and kill Mbutu's "Nephilim King" Nnendi, and destroy his bloodline. An African king of Nephilim lineage would be a devastating blow to the Aryan claim of being the master race due to their angelic ancestry.

The Nazi war machine was referred to as such for a reason, as they cut down lesser equipped forces like a grain harvester, and the Nazi detachment eventually penetrated Mbutu's defenses.

King Nnendi and his wife, Chiwendu, fled to an ally kingdom with their young son, where they acquired traveling documents under the names of Andrew, Wendy, and Nathan.

After escaping to the United States, they lived under their assumed names, keeping their familial lineage a secret from everyone, even their son, who went on to have two sons of his own.

"Nathan was your grandfather," Nana said. "You're a prince."

Sitting back in my chair, I let it all sink in. This was a lot to process. Nephilim? Really? Well, I'd survived a zombie apocalypse, so I guess anything was within the realm of possibility.

Still, it was a lot to take in.

Only days ago I'd been a man condemned to die, and today I learn I'm a prince. Not just a prince, though. A Nephilim prince.

Me!

Crazy!

"With great power comes great responsibility."

My head jerked with her comment. I felt as if she'd seen through me. Like she had read my diary and learned all of my darkest secrets.

"You must be hungry," she said. "Let me go get you guys something to eat."

Nana cooked.

Tristan and I found Sanjay and Brit back at the festival. It was obvious that they'd been having a ball. Both smiling and giggling, I was sure they'd taken a smoke.

"Where were you guys?" Brit asked as we approached.

"We're fine. Just went to go see Nana," I responded.

"Nana?"

"My grandmother," Tristan responded. "She's cooking her jollof rice. You're gonna love it."

"You should meet her. Maybe she can help us understand what's going on between us," I said to Brit.

I could tell they weren't in a hurry to leave the celebration.

To Tristan I asked, "What's the celebration for?"

"A wedding."

"So, what's with the animal masks?" I queried.

"Holbrook is home to the Coven of Lilith. We believe that we are all a part of nature, and without nature there would be no us. Nature is life. Marriage is life. So, we honor one as we honor the other," he explained.

I could understand, and in a way, it was beautiful. The masks were beautiful. Nature was beautiful. Marriage and family were beautiful. Life was beautiful.

Perhaps my second lease on life and freedom made me appreciate things as I never had before.

We entered the house and were assaulted with the pleasant aroma of herbs and spices. Stomach growling like a bear in a rampage, I realized how hungry I really was.

We ate. The company was great, and the food, even better. The festival - and maybe a little something else - had everyone in a joyous mood, and I soaked in the experience.

"Nana," I interrupted. "Brit and I have been having these..."

"Experiences," Brit finished.

"Go on," Nana prompted.

I went on to describe that indomitable pull whenever I looked into Brit's eyes.

"Hmm. I'm not sure," she said. "I'll have to ask some of my sisters and see if they've ever heard of anything like that."

Finished eating, I tried to help Nana clear the table, but she shooed me away.

As Tristan led me to my room for the night, he said, "See. I told you we had plenty of room," before closing the door behind him, leaving me to myself.

As soon as my head hit the pillow, I was out.

Waking early the next morning, I tried sneaking out before anyone woke up, but as I was walking down the street to the stables, Brit came running up behind me.

"You're leaving," she stated.

"I have to go," was all I could come up with.

"Turn around. Look at me."

I turned, the compulsion expressing itself with more intensity than it had last night. Maybe a good night's sleep made it stronger. I was guessing. I still had no idea what to make of this.

"Stay," Brit said. "Don't go."

"I can't."

"Then I'm coming with you," she declared.

"Brit, look... There are things about me that you don't know-
"

She interrupted, "We all have a past. There are many things you don't know about me, too. Nobody's perfect."

"I'm about to do something... dangerous. You can't come. Please, trust me on this. Do not follow me," I pleaded. "I'll come back. I promise."

Brit leaned forward and kissed me. The amount of energy buzzing through me made my knees weak, but her lips were soft and I didn't want it to end, so I locked my knees in place and held her tight, my arms around her waist.

Breaking the kiss, she said, "Promise?"

"You have my word."

She smiled, then headed back toward Nana's house.

I smiled, then went to get Pepper saddled up. Gutenberg wasn't far, and I had a reason to make a hasty return.

10

JASON

Gutenberg was a big city with a big wall, and big oil rigs lined the street leading up to the gate. The wall was so huge, it was hard to imagine that it had been built since the wars. But Gutenberg obviously had the fuel to run heavy machinery in order to get the job done.

As Pepper and I clop-clopped down the road next to a line of cars entering the city, I noticed that guards were posted at regular intervals, protecting the rigs. Oil was an insanely precious commodity, and people were willing to go to war for it.

After entering the city, I noticed more than a few construction projects going on; large cranes lifted steel beams to workers perched high on the skeletons of soon-to-be buildings. Gutenberg was just another modern city, with tall, modern buildings, gas powered vehicles, and people milling about on the sidewalks. The only thing separating this city from modern cities before the war, was that in Gutenberg many people were also traveling by horseback.

The people of Gutenberg were also carrying a lot of steel.

There just weren't many guns around after the wars. After a person had used all of their ammo, they usually tossed the weapon. It just wasn't of any use. No point carrying the extra weight when you might have to outrun a herd of mindless corpses intent on taking a bite out of you.

But, steel... It didn't run out of ammunition. It didn't make a lot of noise, attracting others, both alive and dead. And it was extremely effective.

As I made my way to the city center, it struck me just how many people there were. I'd gotten so used to being alone that I'd forgotten just how crowded cities were. It was an odd thing, seeing this many people when not that long ago I'd been certain that I had met everyone I was going to meet in life.

Parents were chasing after and scolding their children. Couples were holding hands and engaging in public displays of affection. Old men sat in the park playing chess.

Life was happening.

I'd forgotten. I mean, sure, I had memories from my childhood of being around lots of people, but surviving the apocalypse had made you focus on just that: surviving. Then, after, the people left were so scattered about that it was hard to imagine that there were this many people even left in the world.

Taking in the heavily populated city, its inhabitants going on about their daily lives, I thought to myself, *This is going to be just like the beginning of the apocalypse. Just like when my mom died.*

Cookies & cream was my favorite, so that's what I got. The frozen treat was melting, the viscous substance slowly making its way down the cone and onto my hands as we sat at a table in a storefront ice cream shop. Napkins in hand, my mom was fussing over me, constantly wiping my fingers like a sailor scooping water out of a leaky boat to keep from drowning.

Outside, on the street, screams began. Just a few, at first. Then, more screams were layered on top of the others, and it soon sounded as if everyone was screaming.

The glass door exploded inward as someone crashed through it, the glass reminding me of wind chimes as broken shards rained to the linoleum floor.

Rising to his feet, the man looked around the full ice cream shop like a man fresh off a fast would browse a buffet's offerings. Turning to the person nearest, he walked-trotted to her table and took a bite from the side of her neck.

In a panic, the woman clutched her neck as if she could use her hands to plug the wound and staunch the spray of blood squirting through her fingers. But, within seconds, she fell to the floor, lifeless.

Wasting no time, the cannibalistic party crasher- ice cream's always a party, right!- moved on to his next meal, a little boy frozen in fear.

Shaking off her own shock, my mom grabbed me around the waist and dragged me through the shattered entrance and out to the sidewalk.

But, it was even crazier outside.

People were literally running in every direction. It was so chaotic, I couldn't really distinguish chaser from chased. Some people were fighting, others were screaming. Blood was everywhere, and I probably should have spent some time in a therapist's chair afterward, but, you know...

With the Z Wars and death row, and all...

As we ran down the street, a man bumped into my mom. He wasn't one of the crazy people though, so she shoved him off and we kept running. Turning the corner, we weaved through the stalled traffic, bumping into abandoned cars and their open doors, trying to stay as far away from everyone as possible.

A man was exiting an apartment building as we were rushing by, oblivious to the hellish scene before him, and Mom leapt up the three stairs and caught the door just as it was about to close. After racing up a flight of stairs, we sat at the top, my mom cradling me in her arms. Apparently, I was crying because she wiped a tear from my cheek.

She knocked on apartment doors, but no one answered. Maybe nobody was home. Maybe everybody had gotten wind of the madness in the streets and chose not to open their door.

After sunset, she decided that it was as good a time as any to try and get home, so we crept out of the door, into the night.

It was far less chaotic than the daytime had been. The streets looked almost deserted as we scurried along, staying low. A newspaper blew down the street. Somewhere nearby, a cat screeched.

Approaching an alley, we heard a crash. Mom paused, then slowly inched forward to peek around the edge of a building. After having a look, she turned to me with her index finger to her lips for me to keep quiet.

Tiptoeing across the mouth of the alley, I dared a glance. Three people, two guys and a girl, were awkwardly walking in what I would later come to call the walk of the dead. They were facing the opposite direction and posed no threat to us as long as we kept quiet.

Making it home after what seemed like forever, Mom locked all the doors and closed blinds on all of the windows. Then, we went upstairs to her bedroom and locked that door, too.

Lying in my mom's bed, my head on her chest, I slept.

Waking the next morning, I risked a peek out of the window and was greeted with an odd scene. People were just mindlessly, aimlessly wandering the street in blood covered clothes. Some were solitary wanderers, others wandered in groups.

Then, the gunshots began.

Maybe a group of guys got together to take the fight to the dead. There were no shouts, no screams. Just volleys of gunfire.

As Mom and I holed up over the next couple days, that changed.

What had been only gunfire, turned into men shouting commands *and* gunfire. This was followed by men knocking on doors, followed by the explosive sound of men kicking doors open.

Managing to hide inside our house for five days, the sounds of doors being kicked open was alarming. So, we snuck out of our back door before they came kicking down our front door.

After climbing the fence into the backyard of the house directly behind ours, we ran down the side of the house and eased open the gate, exposing the front yard and street. We didn't see any doors that had been kicked off the hinges. The military must have been working in a grid, and had yet to assault this block.

Crossing the street, we ran through the front yard and into the backyard of a house, continuing in this fashion for four more blocks until we came upon a street with a group of zombies lolling about.

Military behind, zombies ahead. The military was a force. Big, armor clad men carrying big, loud guns. The zombies were only a group. I just counted five, and it looked like my mom was thinking the same thing.

Holding my hand, she led me through the front yard and into the street. So intently focused on the dead, she didn't see the set of keys in the middle of the road, kicking them as she took a step.

They didn't make much noise. Just a little tink, tink, ta, tinkle. But, the world without traffic was catacomb silent. The key's brief melody was like an alarm.

Alerted to our presence, the zombies turned in our direction, all five of them.

We ran through the yard into the back, finding ourselves in a narrow alley. Turning left down the alley, we made a right once we reached the street.

At the next corner we encountered another group to our left. Stealth be damned, we zigged and zagged from street to street as the two groups walked-trotted behind us.

Turning down another alley, we made it three quarters of the way down before two more zombies appeared in front of us. We were trapped, the patty and cheese of a zombie burger.

Turning toward me, Mom said, "I'm going to put you in this trash can, then I'm going to lead them away. Be quiet, and don't come out."

She grasped my face between her hands and kissed my forehead, then gave me a hug, crushing me between her arms.

"I love you. Don't come out."

Opening the lid of the trash can, she helped me climb in, then lowered the top.

"Hey, you assholes! Over here!" She yelled. "Hey! Come get it!"

She continued screaming, the volume decreasing with every word, as she led the zombies farther and farther away from me.

PULLING the drone from its bag, I checked the thing out. It wasn't large, maybe a foot square. Crazy that something so small had the power to cause so much death and destruction. Holding it up to the sky, I imagined it flying above the city, releasing its deadly contents.

Infecting the city's inhabitants.

Infecting the children.

How many kids would lose their parents, their protectors, their rocks? How many children would die?

I couldn't do it. I wouldn't do it.

But, I also wasn't looking forward to going back to death row. And why should I? The nation that was willing to spread this virus among thousands of people surely didn't have the moral standing to execute me.

If I went back, that's exactly what would happen, though. There wouldn't be any escaping it.

After returning the drone to its bag I turned Pepper around and headed for the gate. About halfway there, I noticed something in the sky. A speck, sure, but a distinctive speck. Reaching back for my bag, I checked to make sure my drone was still there.

It was.

Ok. That made me feel better, but I still got Pepper up to a trot. Might as well get out of here as soon as possible, anyways.

A sharp pop startled me and I looked up, back toward the sky, checking for that speck.

It wasn't there. It had been replaced by small pieces of falling debris.

And I knew.

Looking around for anyone who looked to be in a rush to leave the city, I saw nothing but life as it should be. No one was alarmed by the drone going all self-destruct, or the falling debris. No one even seemed to notice.

I couldn't get out of here fast enough. Probably wouldn't matter, though. Couldn't outrun those tiny little viral droplets being carried by the wind.

That made me question just how far the virus could travel. Would it reach Holbrook? Would Brit be infected?

As soon as I made it through the gate, I kicked Pepper into a full sprint. Holbrook wasn't far away and I needed to get there ASAP.

11

MIRANDA

A lovely breeze blew through the rooftop garden of the King's Tower. Overlooking Gutenberg, the twenty-one floor building was home to the government of Gutenberg, offices and conference rooms on the lower levels above the Great Hall on the ground floor. The King's residence occupied the upper half of the skyscraper. King Morgain had spared no expense in the appointment of his personal quarters, and the rooftop garden was a reflection of that.

Looking over at the two little children chasing each other around the garden, Princess Miranda said, "Wow, they're getting big. And, Anaya is beautiful. She looks just like you."

"Thanks," Autumn said, brushing her long, auburn braid over her shoulder. "She's a handful. They're both a handful, but Anaya is just like me!"

Autumn giggled. Married to one of the richest men in Gutenberg, one would never know just by looking at her. Preferring cargo pants and hiking boots, she looked as if she'd be more comfortable out in the badlands than in a gown.

She asked, "How's your father? Looks like he's been losing a lot of weight. Is he ok?"

"He refuses to talk about it," the princess responded.

"He's strong" Grabbing Miranda's arm, she said, "So, any guys I should know about?"

"I wish. I just don't have the time. We just hosted a delegation from Eastshore, and we've been negotiating a trade deal. It's just been crazy. But, I don't know. Just haven't met anyone who made me... *feel* something. You know?"

"Let me introduce you to someone," Autumn offered.

"I can't."

"Look, your dad won't be around forever. You're going to need a strong man to solidify your hold on all that your father has built."

"Don't start," Princess Miranda interrupted.

"Just think about it. I know someone who'd be great for you. And he's cute."

Smiling as she shook her head at Autumn's persistence, the princess took a seat on a bench. "He's really cute?"

Hearing it before seeing it, Miranda searched the sky for the drone that was buzzing somewhere near. Although not unheard of, they just weren't a common sight in Gutenberg. Finally locating it, she watched as it seemingly hovered in place, growing smaller, and smaller.

Then, it just blew to pieces. There was no fiery explosion or anything. One moment it was just hovering there, the next it was just debris blowing all over the place. The only indication it had blown was a sharp pop, almost like a balloon bursting.

Unsure what to think, she said, "Let's go inside. Get the children."

As she walked into the tower, her personal guard, Crush, held the door, closing it after everyone was inside.

12

JASON

As soon as I made it through Holbrook's gate, I went straight for Nana's house.

I knocked on the door.

When she answered, I asked, "Where is everybody? Is Brit here?"

"I think they all went out to the gardens," she replied, standing in the doorway.

Without another word, I rushed off, Pepper trotting toward the outskirts of the community. Holbrook's agricultural lands were sizable and it took me a few minutes to find Brit, Tristan, and Sanjay.

Looking up from the weeds she'd been pulling and taking notice of my presence, Brit stood and came to me, a huge smile on her face.

"Hey," she said as she walked up.

"We need to leave. Right now," I started.

"What are you talking about?"

"We gotta get out of here. There's no time to explain every-thing right now, but we *have to* leave," I explained. "I'll tell you everything once we get on the road. Please, Brit."

Sensing the tension, Sanjay and Tristan ambled over.

"What's up, Jason," Sanjay greeted me.

"We gotta get out of here," I responded.

"What are you talking about?" he questioned.

"The virus," I said, giving them something. Didn't look like they were going to budge an inch without some sort of explanation. "It's coming this way."

"Virus?" Tristan piped.

"The Z virus. We're about to have another apocalypse if we don't get out of here."

"How do you know this? Are the dead out there?" Sanjay asked.

"We have to go. Or stay. Your choice. But, it's gonna be bad. So I'm leaving."

"Where are you going?" Brit asked.

"Elan. You coming, or staying?"

"I'm with you," she confirmed.

"Me too," Sanjay followed.

"What the hell," Tristan said. "I'm in."

"Can you get horses?" I asked him.

"Nana's an elder. I can get pretty much whatever we need."

Once their horses had been saddled, we exited the gate and set out north. Toward Elan. The place to which I know without a doubt I shouldn't return. The place where I'll be apprehended and locked back on death row. The place where I'll be executed.

But, Elan had the cure, and I didn't much care to be some zombie's next meal. There's no way to keep the outbreak contained within Gutenberg's wall. Not once it really gets going. The only chance we have is to stop it before it really gets started.

I had to get that cure.

True to my word, I told the small group everything once we were on the road. Everything from that night in the cannabar, my time on death row, to this fool's mission that I'd accepted.

Then, we rode in silence for a long while. I didn't know if they were angry, afraid, or just taking their time processing all that I'd told them.

Then.

"Can we see it?" Brit asked.

"Um... You know there's a live virus in there, right?" I responded.

"You've had it this long and we never knew. We seem to be fine. Unless there's something else you're not telling us."

Touché!

So, we stopped along the side of the road and I gave her the drone.

Taking it from my hand, she flipped it this way and that. Inspecting the drone. Scrutinizing it. At one point she pointed to the small canister beneath the body, looking at me with a question in her eyes.

"That's it." I nodded.

"This little thing is all it takes to end the world?" she asked, almost in disbelief.

"It's kind of anticlimactic, right?" Sanjay said. "You'd think the end of the world would come from some gigantic space blaster, or something."

"Or, an asteroid," Tristan interrupted.

"Right! But, this is just... I don't know. I almost don't even believe it." Sanjay had a point.

To be honest, I couldn't say with absolute certainty that this was what I claimed it was. And the drone that went belly up in Gutenberg... Well, that could have been anything. I hadn't actually *seen* any zombies.

Self-doubt started setting in as I thought about the fact that I'd been on death row only days ago. To be entrusted with such a weapon and relied upon to use that weapon. It *did* seem a little far-fetched.

Then, I thought, *Any more far-fetched than being some angel prince?*

"What are you going to do with it?" Brit asked, bringing me back to the present.

Sanjay said, "You should fly it over Elan, and give them some of their own medicine."

"They have a vaccine," I said, ending that line of thought. "That's why I'm heading back, now."

"You're infected..." Brit wore a concerned look on her face.

"No. I don't know," I stammered. "All those people. Kids. Their parents. I can't... just let them die. I can't."

"So, you're gonna, what? Go all commando and break into the lab? If someone else released the virus, they know you didn't," Tristan said. "You don't think they'll be looking for you?"

"Think about it, Tristan," I responded. "If this gets out of hand, we're going to have the Z Wars all over again. Only this time there aren't that many of us to start with. The other communities and cities won't even know what hit them. Everyone thinks we've won, that the living dead are a thing of the past."

I paused. "We have to stop it before it really gets started. That's the only way."

Silence. Again.

Then, Sanjay said, "We could be heroes. Save the world."

Tristan started laughing, which broke the tension, and we all joined in.

"Heroes... Ok. Let's do it. I'm in," Tristan declared.

Giving the drone back, Brit reached out and took my hand, giving a squeeze as she smiled.

Her touch was electrifying. Literally. The longer I was around her, the more it became a desire. A slight craving. Looking into her eyes, I felt the world starting to slip away.

13

NATE

The day had been a long one, but successful. Now, it was time to relax, have a couple drinks, and a woman.

Nate sat at the ground floor bar of the brothel, one drink down, many more to go.

"Your whore bit my fucking cock," a guy was screaming to the man behind the bar as he pushed a naked woman with fiery hair into the room.

Ignoring the trickle of blood running from the corner of her mouth, she replied, "What he gets. Tried to put his finger up the wrong hole!"

"You're a whore. There is no wrong hole."

"You're the one fucking a whore! Can't get it up for the old lady," she shot back.

The man punched her. Right in the mouth.

Revealing a blood stained smile, she teased, "That all you got? Been hit harder by other whores."

As he raised his hand to strike the woman again, the man behind the bar stepped forward.

"Make to lay your hands on one of my women again, I'll cut

your cock off and let you take a bite yourself." He positioned himself in front of the woman.

"Tell 'im Silk." Then, to the guy, she said, "He's gonna kick your ass something good!"

The man's hand raised, and Nate caught a brief reflection of light on steel.

The edge of a knife was pressed to Silk's throat, his body stiff, every muscle frozen in place to avoid more penetrating contact with the blade.

Slowly rising from his seat, Nate said, "Easy now, soldier. See, I really appreciate whores. But, the thing about whores is that they need fine establishments like this in order to conduct their business. And I was *really* looking forward to enjoying my night here."

The entire time he'd been talking, Nate had been moving closer to the brothel's disgruntled patron.

"I can't do that if you kill the guy that runs the place. So, why don't you put that steel away so we can all get back to it?"

Nate laid his hand on the guy's shoulder, all buddy-buddy like. As the guy turned, focusing on the offending hand, Nate used his other hand to slide a blade of his own between the man's ribs, piercing his liver.

Surprise registered on the guy's face as he looked down at the hilt of the knife protruding from his side.

Taking advantage of the distraction, Silk backed away from his would-be killer's knife, grabbing the bloody whore in the process, and disappearing into the back.

Pain finally registered on the man's face as Nate removed the blade from his flesh. There was a surprisingly small amount of blood, but that was the thing with liver wounds. They bleed internally. You never really know how bad the damage is.

Clutching his side, the man dragged himself across the room and out the door.

Good riddance.

"Fuck, Nate. You're having all the fun today," Yoshi said as he combed his fingers through his long, blond hair. "First, you get to fly the drone. Now, this. Lucky bastard."

"The drone was business. This is pleasure," Nate replied. "He was ruining my evening. But he won't be anymore."

"You're gonna lead an army. Gotta learn how to delegate. Spread the fun around. You can't be the entire army."

Nate said, "Maybe you're right. But it's not official yet. And don't you ever forget. I *am* an army."

Raising their drinks, the two men drank and laughed.

Returning from the back, Silk approached Nate and said, "Drinks are on the house. A woman, too. Pick whichever one you like. I owe you a debt of gratitude."

Spotting a dark haired beauty with brown, almond shaped eyes, Nate tilted his head in her direction and said, "Her."

Silk summoned, and she sauntered over. Her walk was honey, slow and fluid. Her eyes were fire, all lust and seduction.

Laying a hand on Nate's chest, she said, "That was very brave of you."

Speaking to Yoshi, Nate said, "I think I like this one." Then, slapping him on the shoulder, "Catch you later."

After leading Nate up the stairs and into a room, she said, "Be right back."

Returning a minute later with a bottle of whiskey and two cups, she poured drinks and sat on the edge of the bed.

"You're cute," she said.

"Flattery will get you everywhere, love. What's your name?"

"Alma."

"A fine name for a beautiful woman."

"Silk told me to make sure you were well taken care of."

"Did he, now?"

"But, he didn't have to tell me," she said, taking his mostly empty glass and sitting it on a table next to the bed.

Pushing him back onto the soft mattress, Alma climbed on top and planted kisses on his stomach as she raised his shirt.

At long last, the relaxation part of this evening had finally begun.

~

YOSHI DOWNED A COUPLE MORE DRINKS, then realized he needed to take a leak. There was a bathroom inside the brothel, but he'd always found something liberating about using a good, old-fashioned tree.

Stepping outside to pursue his urinary preference, Nate crossed a small lot to a copse. Finding a satisfactory trunk, he went about his business, closing his eyes and raising his head to the heavens.

A rustle of leaves off to his left caught his attention, and Yoshi's head whipped in the direction of the sound.

Bastard's coming back for more, he thought, recognizing the man that Nate had just stabbed.

Putting himself away and drawing a dagger, Yoshi faced the man and felt something was off.

First off, the man was walking weird. More a lurch with a shuffle than what you'd consider a stride.

"Want a piece of me this time around?" Yoshi called out to no response.

The man just continued his lurch, inching closer and closer within range of attack.

Yoshi lunged, driving his dagger deep into the man's stomach.

But the man kept coming, unaffected.

Driving his blade into the man's belly over and over, Yoshi started to feel the first tingling of fear crawling up his spine.

Fuck! Bastard just keeps coming.

Now carrying all of the man's weight, he shoved a forearm

into the attacker's throat as the man began snapping his teeth like a rabid dog.

Backing into a tree he thought, *Not gonna die in my own piss.*

Bringing his dagger up high, he shoved it into the side of the snarling head. That did the job. The man fell to the ground.

Dead. Again.

Running back into the brothel, Yoshi took the stairs two at a time, crashing through the door of Nate's room.

Sitting astride Nate, the woman startled at Yoshi's entrance, but never stopped the rhythmic sway of her hips.

"The fuck you want," Nate boomed.

"That guy you killed... I just killed him again." Yoshi's chest heaved as he spoke.

"You're shitting me," Nate said, as he tossed the woman to the side.

"Wish I was."

"We need to contact Command. I'd planned on making them wait 'til morning, but... Let's go," Nate said, pulling on his pants and shoes.

14

THE GERENT

Rising from his desk, Gerent Malbent welcomed Vicar into his office. Due to meet about the success of the Gutenberg mission, he couldn't wait to give Vicar the news.

As soon as they were seated, he said, "I have wonderful news. The virus has been successfully disbursed, and it is effective. We've had reports from the field of an encounter with an infected already."

"That is great news," Vicar said. "Except, only one drone was deployed. Looks to me like someone has gone off of the reservation."

"Even so, the mission was still accomplished. That's why we sent two teams, instead of one."

"Your mission was a failure. You're their leader, and you can't control your charges. Not only are you responsible for the successes, but the failures as well. Now, there's some loose end out there running around with the apocalypse in a can. A loose end who can tell the world that your nation released it. You call that a success? An accomplishment? You disappoint me, Jefferson," Vicar scolded.

Looking deflated, the Gerent stood and went to the window.

He looked out. Turning back around to address Vicar, he said, "I'll take care of it."

"How exactly do you plan on doing that?"

"I have someone."

"Your little angel, or Nephilim, or whatever? Has he even come into his powers, yet?"

"He has," Malbent confirmed, taking his seat again.

"Fine. Just make sure he retrieves the canister. By The One, we don't need that thing floating around out there."

A knock on the door, then it opened a crack as a head popped in.

The head said, "Dean Wilson, sir."

"Send him in," the Gerent ordered.

Entering the room, the bags under Dean's eyes were apparent, exhaustion covering his body like a blanket.

"You look like shit, Dean," Vicar pointed out.

"Feels like I've been riding that damned horse forever. I need a hot shower and my bed," he responded.

"How was your trip?" Malbent asked.

"Eastshore was a waste of time. They practically laughed in my face when I told them that the virus was coming."

Dean paused, a smile appearing on his face. "But the Highlanders are going to play ball. They were gracious and welcoming, almost suspiciously so, but their soldiers should be a couple days behind me."

"Should we divert some of their troops toward Eastshore?" Vicar asked.

"That might be a good idea," Dean replied. "Maybe a mixed force, with some of our guys sprinkled in. We don't want to have a completely foreign force at our six, defending us from another foreign force that they could potentially link up with."

"Agreed," said the Gerent. "Do our troops have everything they need?"

"McClendon gave us sufficient funding before I left. He's

been on board since the beginning, and I'm sure that if something comes up and we need more, he'll make sure we have it." Dean stood and stretched. "I have to get some rest. If anything comes up while I'm asleep, don't bother me. Please."

"Dean," the Gerent said. "Sit back down for a moment. We may have a problem."

Malbent explained that only one drone had been deployed, although the mission had been successful, nonetheless.

"Give Nate Alexander your best men to track down Jason Alexander, and bring us his head," Vicar added. "Too much of a risk to keep him alive. He was already condemned to die, and we tried to give him a second lease at life, but he spat in our faces. He'll get no more reprieves. He made his choice. Find him immediately! Once he comes into his power, it's going to be almost impossible to stop him, and that should be happening soon. Nate has already begun experiencing his, and he's less than a year older than Jason."

He paused. "Thank The One, Nate is one of us. "

Sitting with a confused look on his face, Dean asked, "Power? What exactly are we talking about here?"

The Gerent responded, "These guys are Angels. Or, at least, descendants of Angels. Nephilim."

Rubbing both hands down his face, Dean said, "You're fucking with me, right? I'm too tired for this shit."

Vicar asked, "Do you not believe in the supernatural, Dean?"

"No. I believe what my eyes see, not some gobbledygook about super powers and angels."

"Then, how do you explain the Z Wars? The Apocalypse? Everything that's led us to this very moment?" Vicar asked.

"Science. The apocalypse was caused by a virus, a micro-organism. This... What you're saying... It's crazy!"

"If I had come to you fifteen years ago and told you that the world would be destroyed by flesh eating zombies, would you have thought that crazy, as well?" Vicar smoothed his robes as he spoke.

"Yes. I would have thought you were a raving lunatic," Dean answered.

"Yet, it happened. Right before your very eyes," Vicar said. "The fact that you haven't seen something isn't proof of its non-existence. You've witnessed what you'd previously thought impossible. Now is not the time to doubt."

Dean quietly sat there for a moment. Then, he said, "Tell you what, I'll sleep on it. How about that?" Standing, he started walking toward the door. "Remember. Don't bother me."

As soon as the door closed behind Dean, Vicar said, "I'm only going to say this once, so listen closely. Don't let your ambition get bigger than your capabilities. You thought having two Nephilim under your wing would allow you to wield enough power to take me on, but I have eyes everywhere. The One has blessed me with his omniscience, so I know all."

Looking around his desk, at the carpet, toward the window, anywhere but Vicar's eyes, Malbent said, "It wasn't like that. I've known Nate since the wars, since he was a kid. And, if Jason had come into the fold. I mean, can you imagine the both of them leading our army? No one could stop us."

"But, now, all you have is a big pile of horse shit to clean up. Get it done."

Rising from his seat, Vicar straightened his robes and exited the office, leaving the Gerent to himself.

15

MIRANDA

Waking early for a morning run was a habit that she'd developed after the wars, mainly because she could. The dead had been eradicated, cities were being built. The word "safe" was beginning to have meaning again, and morning runs became Miranda's way of exploring this newfound safety.

Being the princess, two guards trailed as she ran through the streets of downtown Gutenberg. A few vehicles cruised the streets, and she dodged a handful of pedestrians who were groggily heading toward their destinations.

Up ahead, she noticed traffic was backed up, which struck her as crazy, since there wasn't any traffic to speak of this early in the morning.

But, stalled traffic it was.

Shuffling between the lanes, she swerved around cars until coming alongside the vehicle that was holding everyone up. The first thing Miranda noticed was the blood on the inside of the window.

Noticing the red splatter just as she did, Crush jumped ahead, shielding her from any threat that could possibly come from that little black car. The other guard stepped forward, warily opening the door to see if any help could be offered to the injured. But as the latch released, a sudden bump from inside the door caused the guard to lose his balance.

The zombie was all over him as it crawled out of the car.

Miranda's heart fell to the ground, opening a deep pit in her stomach, and she felt like they'd fought the wars for nothing. It'd been years, but the ugly bastards were still around.

Inside her city.

Muscle memory kicking in, Crush stepped forward, drawing his dagger, and planting it right into the side of the zombie's head.

Rolling from beneath his de-animated attacker, the guard searched his body for bites. Once the adrenaline was flowing, a person could easily not notice an injury, so he conducted a thorough search, and – *damn it!* - found a small bite on the back of his arm.

Crush and Miranda looked on in horror, not knowing what to do. Gutenberg had a stockpile of the vaccine and antiviral, but everyone had been inoculated and should have immunity. Unless...

Unless, the virus had mutated.

Turning to Crush, she said, "Let's get to the hospital and get him started on a round of antivirals. His vaccination should make him immune, but just in case he isn't, we need to try to kill anything that was passed along through that bite."

Nodding in agreement, Crush helped him back to his feet, and the guard dusted himself off with an embarrassed look on his face.

"I'm fine, I'm fine," the guard said. "I've done every round of vaccinations recommended. Took the anti-viral to kill off the initial virus. I'm good, guys. Seriously."

"Everyone has," she replied, then pointed to the man on the ground. "I'm sure he had, too. As my personal guard, your job is to protect me - and you did an awesome job just now. But if this virus has mutated, your vaccinations won't work. You have to go to the hospital, or into quarantine."

"Hospital it is," he replied.

Walking into the hospital, Miranda was in complete disbelief. There were about two dozen bite victims lounging around the waiting room, all minor bites, but bites nonetheless.

This wasn't right. Couldn't be. She briefly wondered if maybe the vaccines that everyone had received were only temporary. Maybe antibodies that built up slowly metabolized after not coming into contact with what they were meant to fight, leaving the immune system susceptible to re-infection after a period of time.

"We're all going to die," said a woman with salt and pepper hair pulled back into a ponytail. "We're *all* going to die. The world shall answer for its wickedness. Fire and brimstone shall rain down upon the earth and smite the wicked! The dead shall rise and inherit the earth!"

"Quit your yappin', lady!" a man shouted back from the corner of the waiting room. "Or, I've got a mind to come over there and quit it for you!"

But, she continued, giving her passionate sermon of fire and brimstone to the increasingly crowded waiting room. Not that her preaching was doing anything to help. Actually, it had the opposite effect.

People were already nervous due to the fact that they'd been bitten in the first instance, when the Z virus was supposed to have been eradicated. Destroyed. A distant memory. Then, out of nowhere, they wake up this particular morning to people trying to take a bite out of them.

She briefly thought back to the drone exploding over the city yesterday then quickly shook the thought away.

Miranda was surprised that the waiting room hadn't already erupted into complete chaos. Maybe something to do with the stages of grief, the first being disbelief. This wasn't exactly grief, but it was a situation that many would find hard to accept. After surviving one apocalypse, we're dealing with another just a few years later? Yeah, that could be a hard pill to swallow.

Miranda's guard was taken into the back to receive treatment ahead of everyone else due to his status as Royal Guard. There were a couple of grunts in response to his jumping ahead of everyone, but for the most part, Princess Miranda's privilege was taken in stride.

Making her way around the room, she tried to give comfort to those who were freaking out, and just talked to others. She'd always prided herself on how she connected with the people of Gutenberg. At her core, she was just like everyone else. Not born to royalty, or with a silver spoon in her mouth. Her dad, King Morgain, had been the foreman of a crew of roughnecks working a rig in the gulf when the world ended. Losing her mother to cancer at a young age, Miranda clung to her father's side, surviving, until happening upon this oil rich land near the end of the wars.

And Morgain knew oil. He was also a natural leader. So, Gutenberg rose from the ashes, built on the need for fuel, and Morgain's innate leadership shaped that need into a prosperous city-state.

Approaching a man who was obviously not doing well, Miranda called out to the woman sitting behind the desk checking patients into the clinic, "Nurse! This guy needs help. Hey! He's dying right in front of you!"

Ignoring Miranda's urgent tone, the overworked nurse was trying to keep everything organized with the influx of patients while dealing with her own fear. Being surrounded by people who'd been bitten by the dead was a direct path to her own death, and she was barely holding it together.

"I know you hear me! This man needs help!"

"The only help he's gonna need is a blade to the brain, by the looks of him," Crush said. "He'll be turning any minute. Look at the color of his skin. See how gray it is? That's how I could always tell when they were about to turn. A man who dies normal doesn't turn this color. We need to be leaving, my Princess."

"I need to speak with father," Miranda said, already heading for the door.

Back at the tower, Miranda and Crush rode the elevator to King Morgain's penthouse chambers, where he was getting dressed and going over the day's agenda with one of his assistants.

"Morning, sweetie," the King said, noticing his daughter's arrival in the room, as well as the distressed look on her face. "What's wrong?"

"They're back, dad. It's started all over again."

"Sweetie, you need to be a little more specific than that. What are you talking about?"

"Your Highness," Crush interrupted. "The dead are walking again."

Looking at his daughter, the King said, "Is this true?"

"Yes, dad. Gerald," she spoke of her other guard, "was bitten this morning, and when we took him to the clinic, there were a couple dozen more. All bite victims."

"And, you're sure they are zombies?"

"Crush had to take his blade to the damned thing's head," Miranda confirmed.

To the assistant, King Morgain said, "Get my cabinet to the conference room, immediately." Then, to Miranda, "Start locking down the city. Implement the social distancing protocols and get everyone indoors. Anyone needs a weapon, make sure they get it."

"Dad," she interrupted.

"How could this have happened? I thought we were done with this." The King spoke with an exasperated tone.

"Dad, that's what I'm trying to tell you. I was in the garden yesterday and saw a drone explode-"

"And you didn't tell me," the King barked.

"It wasn't like that. Not really an explosion like you're thinking. It just... broke. Like it flew into a wall, or something. It was nothing, at the time. But with what's going on this morning, it's just too much to be a coincidence."

"Be careful what you say."

"It's the only thing that makes sense. How often do you see drones flying?" Miranda asked.

"Drones need batteri-" Cutting himself off, King Morgain cursed. "Fucking Elan, and their piece of shit Gerent. That bastard, Malbent, had been trying to get me to sell them oil at thirty percent off market value. That's robbery! And he's been in his feelings since I refused him." Dressed, he took off for the elevator to the conference room.

"You think he did this," Miranda asked, trying to keep up with his fast pace.

"They have the most advanced battery technology in the known world. Everyone else is using gas, or steam. I'm certain of it. This was an act of war. Damn good strategy, too. Let us eat each other within these walls, then come and clean up after. Shit would have been cake."

Being first to arrive in the conference room, King Morgain took his seat at the head of the table. "Go, now, Miranda. Get the city locked down."

Nodding her head, she turned to leave, Crush close on her heels. Reaching the door, she heard her father call out, "If you see Jazz, tell her I need some coffee!"

16

JASON

Smoke rose from the campfires, alerting our small group to the presence of someone up ahead. Motioning for everyone to move into the tree line next to the road we'd been walking alongside, I brought Pepper to a halt once we were out of sight.

"That's too much smoke for one campfire, and I don't remember any communities around here from the ride down," I said.

"There's a village to the east," Tristan said. "But it should be a straight shot to Elan from here."

"So, what do you think," Sanjay asked, looking in my direction.

"Could be anything. We'll keep quiet and go slow until we get closer."

Then, the smell of wood smoke was upon us, and we dismounted. Noises reached my ears, although we were still too far away for specifics. But we were close enough that I felt the need to send a scout.

And I just had a feeling.

During the wars, and thereafter, I'd learned to trust my gut.

Maybe being the prey to some predatory zombie's hunger had honed a primal instinct deep within me, but I'm alive because of it.

And I trust it.

"I'll go," Brit volunteered.

"No," I countered.

"Yes. I'm part of this team, not some damsel in distress you need to hover over. I'm the smallest, lightest, and the quietest. I got it."

Brit ran off and disappeared as the late afternoon sun pierced the dense overhang in places, creating arrow-straight beams of light.

Tristan, Sanjay, and I found a downed tree and sat on its trunk, drinking water. After some time had passed, I started to worry. Silently slipping into the trees, I went looking for her, my two traveling companions watching until I disappeared.

Unfair to both of us, I'd been feeling responsible for Brit's safety. I felt guilty for even coming to look for her, like she couldn't get the job done. That's absolutely *not* what I was thinking, but that guilt persisted, mixed with a good amount of worry. Chalking it up to the magnetism we shared, I pushed on, moving as silently as possible across the dry twigs and decaying leafs that carpeted the earth.

A hand from behind clamped over my mouth and pulled me to the ground behind a large bush with small, dark fruit ornamenting its thin branches. Panic attempted to seize control of my body, causing my heart to beat wildly in my chest. Energy flowed beneath my skin, its buzzing intensity as strong as it had ever been. Until I realized that the hand covering my mouth was quite small. Looking down I saw an arm that had been kissed a golden brown by the sun and her rich ancestry.

Brit.

Immediately relaxing, I sank to the forest floor beside the bush.

Sensing that I'd calmed, she removed her hand, allowing me to turn my head and look into her eyes. Holding a finger to her lips, Brit nodded in the direction that I had been heading.

Then I heard it, the soft crunch of twigs snapping beneath a foot. Multiple feet. Almost barreling right into a group of men, I'd been saved by the person I had been coming to check on.

The guilt came back tenfold.

After the group had passed, we raised our heads above the bush in search of visual confirmation.

All clear.

"What are you doing here?" She asked in a harsh whisper.

"Was looking for you," I replied.

"You almost got us caught." We stood and started back in the direction from which I'd come. "There's a whole army out there. We're going to have to sneak around them."

"Where are they going?"

"I don't know," she shot back. "Nowhere. They're just sitting around, for the most part. A couple are out, but that's it. Should be easy enough to get around them as long as we stay quiet."

Before making it back to Tristan and Sanjay, she led me down another path, in another direction, away from our companions. "Come on," she said.

I followed. Was happy to. We really hadn't had a moment to ourselves, so consumed with everything that had been going on, and this was a welcome change in direction.

Breaking free of the trees, we emerged in a meadow, high grass and brightly colored flowers blanketing the landscape. Bees flitted from flower to flower as hummingbirds beat their wings at an invisible pace, hovering in front of blossoms and devouring the nectar before moving on to the next.

A peach tree had taken root at the edge of the meadow, its fruit swollen and ripe. Pulling two from the tree, I gave one to Brit and took a bite from the other.

"When I was a girl, before the wars, my dad would take me

to his friend's house out in the country. His friend had a son that was my age. Kanye. He had this wild, crazy afro," Brit said with a chuckle. "And, out on their land there was a meadow. Just like this." She spread her arm across the field.

"Being from DC, you just never saw this much space, so every time we went to visit, Kanye and I would go out to the field and race-"

"Race?" I interrupted.

"What! I'd leave him in the dust," she bragged.

"Nope. I don't believe it."

Snatching my half eaten peach from my hand, Brit held it up, said, "Want it? Come and get it!"

She took off at a sprint, into the middle of the meadow.

I gave chase. What can I say? I was hungry.

Quick as a cat, Brit dodged around me, left and right, cutting this way and that. I had to admit it, she was fast. But, I could have caught her at any time. I was enjoying myself too much, though. Felt like a kid again. To just run, and laugh, and be free. I'd done too little of that in my life.

Finally catching up to Brit, I wrapped my arms around her and we both fell to the ground, disappearing into the soft grass, my body cushioning her fall.

She stared into my eyes, and I felt it. That compulsion. She must have felt it as well, because her lips pressed against mine, and the world slipped away. We were everywhere and nowhere at the same time. We were everything, and nothing, and time had ceased to exist.

Chaste at first, the kiss grew warmer, hungry, with more urgency. Our tongues met and danced a tango, spinning and dipping. Twirling and crossing.

WE MADE it back to Tristan and Sanjay as the day turned to night. They had foraged a variety of berries, and we snacked as we formed our plan to get past the troops.

Leading our horses by the reins, we headed out north, toward the troops, and then Elan. The sounds of camp grew as we closed in, which was a good thing as it would help mask any noise we made.

Brit had scouted a spot that, if we were lucky and timed it right, we could slip right through their camp, saving us from having to go all the way around the detachment.

The camp narrowed to a bottleneck, and we hid in the trees to wait for an officer, dressed in his blue uniform, and his aide to pass us by.

"The biggest problem will be breaking through that damned wall. I'll not be camped out for the next year waiting on them to break siege..." The officer's voice trailed off as they moved past.

Then, it was clear. Reins in hand, we crossed the narrow patch of field, our horses trailing behind, and soon we were into the trees on the other side of the camp.

Still taking things slowly, we'd made about five hundred yards past the camp when we stumbled across a soldier who had been relieving himself behind a tree.

Startled, he hurriedly pulled his pants up and drew a sword, which told me that he was a foot soldier, a private, so to speak. The advanced weapons were reserved for the higher ranking officers and special detachments, unless one had the means to purchase their own weapons. Which was rare among the commoners.

"Halt!" he called out.

Hand moving toward the Scythe, I said, "We're just passing through, not looking to cause any trouble. We'll just be on our way, now."

"Stop! Don't move!" He was persistent.

Pulling a device from the pocket of his green uniform with his free hand, the screen came to life and he glanced at it briefly. "You're Jason Alexander. Wanted by the Nation of Elan for murder and treason. We've been ordered to take you into custody on si-"

His body tensed, cutting his words off mid-speech, and he fell to the ground, unconscious. The only warning had been the soft puff of air from the Scythe as it released its cartridge, but he'd been so caught up in his monologue that he'd never have been able to pick up on it.

Walking to his limp body, I pulled the cartridge from his flesh, grabbing the device he'd been looking at with my other hand. The others gathered around as I brought the glowing screen up to eye level.

My face was plastered on the screen, a recent picture, taken after my midnight visit from Agent Mays, and my acceptance of his offer. Below my beautiful mug were the basic biographical information, age, height, weight, and the reason for my detainment, which was exactly as stated by the soldier.

Treason and murder.

"Well, it's not quite untrue," Sanjay said.

"Can those be tracked?" Tristan asked.

I didn't know. None of us knew.

Leaving the device behind, we continued on. The clear sky allowed the light of the moon to guide our way, and we made good progress. Not wanting to camp anywhere close to the military detachment, we traveled for most of the night, staying off of the main roads and thoroughfares in favor of game trails.

As we were stopped for a restroom break, Brit looked up suddenly, said, "Do y'all hear that?"

Feeling it before I heard it, the hoof beats of a group of horses being rode hard filtered to me just as Tristan began yelling.

"Riders! Come on. We gotta go!"

Mounting our horses, we kicked the powerful beasts into gear and stormed off into the night, dodging low hanging branches as we rode. I had no idea how many riders were behind us, and I didn't much care to find out.

Someone must have found the unconscious lad. Or, maybe the effects of the tazing had worn off and he'd groggily rushed back to sound the alarm.

I guess at this point it really didn't matter. We were on the run and there was no way we could let them catch us.

Us.

It wasn't just me in this mess. A group of people had decided to come with me, at my prodding, not fully understanding the situation. That was my fault, and I couldn't allow these people to come to harm on my behalf.

Especially since I hadn't been completely honest from the beginning.

Hearing a yelp from behind, I turned around to find Sanjay falling through the air as his horse toppled to the ground. Bringing Pepper around to go back and help him, I saw a cartridge protruding from the rear of the horse.

Brit and Tristan had turned back as well, and were right behind me as I hopped down and plucked the cartridge from the beast's flesh.

"Get down," I called out. "At least one of them has a Scythe."

Their feet touched the ground just as the first rider came into view.

Firing up the e-spear, I stepped forward, blocking the rider's path. The brightly glowing arc suddenly illuminating the night caused the rider's horse to pull up, throwing him from the saddle and obstructing the trail so that the other riders couldn't pass.

He rose to his feet, and I saw steel in his hand. He must have dropped the Scythe in his fall. Charging at me like an enraged bull, he swung his sword, trying to take my head with one fell blow.

Raising the e-spear to block his attack, I angled the shaft so the arc would make contact with his blade.

Live and you learn, right?

The shock bit him, but he didn't immediately release his weapon. He froze, stiff, the electricity grabbing hold of him and not letting go. Which wasn't necessarily a good thing for me.

Another rider was dismounting to join the fight.

Sanjay had regained his footing and held a long dagger in his hand. Rushing to take the second attacker before he could reach me, Sanjay caught him off guard and drove the dagger into the man's side. Mesmerized by his friend's response to the blade's contact with the e-spear, he never even saw Sanjay until it was too late.

After helping him to his feet, Brit stood next to where Sanjay had been, hands empty, watching things unfold.

Killing the e-spear, I let the man fall to the ground, then unsheathed the machete I'd taken when I first met her. I tossed it to Brit, her nimble fingers wrapping around the shaft as she caught it.

Three more men ran up and Tristan joined the fight, holding a curved blade with strange markings etched into its surface.

Then, an e-spear appeared, the first I'd encountered other than my own. It was carried by a soldier in a blue uniform. An officer. He swung in a wide loop, and I caught it with mine, but he was strong and the arc crackled so close to my face that I could feel the short hairs of my beard standing up.

Twisting under his spear, I stepped to the outside and sliced the arc across his spear arm, severing it to the aroma of searing flesh. Surprise registered on his face until he looked down and saw the damage. Then, he released a howl worthy of an alpha wolf.

As more men surrounded us, I saw Brit struck down from the corner of my eye. A soldier had parried her machete, delivering a massive punch to the abdomen with his fist. She doubled over in pain before falling to her knees. The man raised his own blade above his head to deliver the fatal blow.

The buzzing compulsion kicked up to a level I hadn't experienced before. I turned toward them, running to get there before he brought his blade down, but I didn't make it.

It *felt* like I'd made it, but my body never moved. It was an out-of-body experience.

The man flew, crashing into the tree behind him with so much force that his still-raised blade lodged itself into the trunk.

The fighting paused for a moment as everyone stared at the man on the tree. Then, I guess everyone realized they were still in a fight, and the action continued.

We were outnumbered, though. There was no way we'd win this fight in this fashion. I needed to do again what I'd just done.

But I had no idea how I'd done it. Not really a conscious thing, it just happened. And, to top it off, I didn't even know what exactly it was that I'd done.

I knew how it felt, though.

Focusing on the feeling, I tensed up, trying to make the energy flow.

Nothing.

Nada.

Zilch.

Then, another guy just waltzed right up to me, e-spear in hand. Taunting me as I raised mine, he swung his spear.

I blocked it, but he was coming strong. Barely able to get an attack in, I backpedaled with each of his attacks. Not only was he good, he was powerful. Fast, as well.

He was beating my ass.

Brit must have noticed, too, because she ran over to help, swinging her machete and cutting him across the side of his abdomen.

He looked down at the wound, then up at her, all composed and undaunted. Then, he backhanded her across the face.

It happened again, even stronger this time. The out-of-body experience pulled at me, only this time I didn't focus on one person, in one direction. I spread my focus wide, tried to feel it all around me.

As my out of body experience raced in every direction, men were tossed backward and fell. All of them.

Except, the guy I'd been fighting. Slightly taller than I, an odd look crossed his face as he ran a hand across his short, wavy hair.

Sanjay was first to attack him, followed by Brit. Soon, all four of us were slashing and stabbing, swinging and thrusting, trying to fell him.

Holding on for as long as he could, the man blocked and parried, moved and countered, but in the end, he retreated.

Wasting no time, our quartet stepped around all of the downed soldiers, mounted our horses, and raced off into the night, trying to put as much distance between us and them as possible.

17

JASON

The house and stables came into view through the early morning fog. We were exhausted; the night had been long. We rode hard, not stopping, our mounts drenched in sweat.

"They're not gonna stop looking for us. You know that, right?" Tristan said. "What are we going to do?"

"We're going to get the cure and take it to Gutenberg. Maybe we can save all of those people before Elan's army attacks."

"You should go west. Into the badlands," Sanjay piped. "They'll never look for you there."

"I'm not running," I stated. "Letting all of those people die is just the same as me releasing that virus myself. I could have lived happily ever after. But we all lost people during the wars. I know I did. And if I had the chance to go back and stop it before it started, I would in the blink of an eye. I'm getting that cure back to Gutenberg."

"*We're* gonna do it," said Brit.

Tristan agreed, "Damned right we are!"

"But how?" Sanjay queried. "Do you even know where it is? And how are we going to get into wherever they keep it?"

"Hopefully, with a little help," I said, turning onto the gravel drive of Agent Reece's horse ranch.

There was a possibility that I was wrong about this being her place, but what other choice did I have? Storming the lab would be suicide, and that's as counterproductive as it gets. No, someone had to get me in. That would be the only way.

Reece had been very familiar with the horses, I remembered. And no one else had been around. Either this was her place, or she spent a good amount of time here.

Riding past the house, we saw Agent Reece in front of the stable entrance with a young man, his longish, blond hair falling across his eyes.

She spoke to him and he turned into the gloominess of the stables.

"You're a wanted man, Jason," she called out as we approached.

"We need to talk," I said in response.

"Or I could just have my nephew radio in for backup, and we take you into custody."

"You obviously know that I didn't do what I was sent to do," I said. "And if you haven't already told him to call it in, that tells me you don't necessarily disagree with my decision."

"You really shouldn't be here," said Reece.

Climbing down from Pepper, I pleaded, "Please. Just hear me out. What did you mean when you said I was different?"

"Nate is... ambitious. He wants the glory, the power," she began. "But you didn't seem impressed that the Gerent had personally given you this mission."

"Who's Nate?"

"Your cousin. Don't you know him? Your fathers were brothers."

I didn't know that my father had a brother, or that I had a cousin.

"I don't understand," I stammered.

"Haven't you wondered why you were chosen for this mission? Any number of people would have quickly taken this on." Agent Reece leaned against a post next to the stable's entrance. "Especially from death row. But you of all people were chosen. Why is that?"

"I don't know," I admitted.

"You're special. Both you and your cousin, Nate. You carry the messenger gene-"

"What's that?" I interrupted.

"It's called the messenger gene because Angels were the messengers of God. You carry their DNA. We actually matched your DNA to your grandfather, whose power was well documented. You and Nate were meant to lead Elan's army as the Gerent tries to reunite this land. Nate's leading the assault on Gutenberg."

"You have to help us."

"That's what I'm doing," she responded.

"No," I said. "We need to get the cure back to Gutenberg."

"No way. Not happening."

Tristan stepped forward. "My community isn't far from Gutenberg. We don't have a military. If the virus spreads into my community it will kill so many people. Please. You have to help us. You have to help save my community."

"What do you want me to do?" she asked.

"Get us inside," I said. "And tell us where to go. We'll do the rest."

"If I get caught..."

"If you don't help us, people will die. We're talking about thousands of lives here. That's worth the risk."

Brit asked, "What kind of power did his grandfather exhibit?"

"He could move things with his mind," Reece responded. "He was also known to control people's minds. But, it was more like he made strong suggestions that people couldn't disobey." She turned toward me. "Have you begun to exhibit any powers yet?"

I nodded my head, yes. "How do I control it?"

"I don't know. Just relax and it'll come. You were made for it. But you do know that if you get caught they're going to kill you," Agent Reece said.

"Well, I've been a dead man walking for the past 5 years. At least if I die, I'll die doing something worth dying for."

"Ok," she said, reluctantly. "I'll help. Start working on that mind control thing. It can come in handy."

"Mike," she screamed toward the stable entrance. "It's ok. You can come out."

Mike emerged, warily looking from face to face.

"I'm going to help them," she said to the young man. "If I'm not back by tomorrow morning, pack up and get to the lake house. Ok?"

Mike nodded, offering us a small smile.

18

THE GERENT

Answering Vicar's summons, Gerent Malbent entered the dimly lit altar room. Candle light created a dance of shadows upon the wall, the quivering flames bobbing back and forth as Vicar knelt before their quiet brilliance.

"You failed again," he boomed at the Gerent. "Your incompetence amazes me. You had an entire army out there and they couldn't take one man! And your wonder boy, Nate, let a group of undisciplined misfits run him off. You're worthless. If I didn't need you to be the public face of this nation, I'd kill you right now."

Vicar paused as Malbent received his chastisement in silence.

"Since I must be the one to do everything, I'll take care of this little problem myself."

Grabbing a knife from the floor and unsheathing it, Vicar cut his hand, allowing the blood to drip into a bowl filled with an assortment of ingredients used to call upon magic. After lighting a match and dropping it into the bowl, bringing about a bright flash and puff of smoke, he took the bowl and poured its contents over a small mound of earth.

The Gerent had obviously heard of magic, but being the discerning man he was, thought it to be foolish stories told to children to keep them entertained. But being in the presence of Vicar as he began chanting in a strange language made Malbent feel extremely uncomfortable. Anxious, even.

Vicar's melodic chanting grew louder, and as it did, the light emanating from the candles intensified, growing brighter with the intensity of his voice.

The green veins of the honored orb pulsed and throbbed, creating an illusionary effect that was almost three dimensional.

The mound of earth before Vicar began to shift and move, its shapeless mass starting to take form. The shape of a baby appeared, then it rapidly grew into a toddler. Within minutes the cycle of adolescence to adulthood had been completed, and before Vicar stood a man, fully grown.

Extremely misshapen and deformed, the creature had the structure and build of a man, but lacked defined facial features, having only impressions of eyes, nose, and mouth. Standing over seven feet tall, the beast was huge, as well as girthy, its chest worthy of Mr. Olympian status. With massive hands more likely to be thought of as mitts, the creature beat its chest as it lifted its face toward the heavens.

"Jefferson," Vicar said. "I'd like you to meet the Guardian."

Guardians of The One were molded from clay and given life through magic. Almost indestructible, Guardians protected their conjurers instinctually, and were also controlled by those who brought them to life.

Malbent was incredulous. This thing had come to life right in front of his eyes. Sure, Nephilim and Angels were of the supernatural, but, this was... Different. Almost wrong, even. Like Vicar was playing at being a god, creating life from nothing.

Vicar said a few words in the strange language he'd been chanting, and the Guardian moved toward the Gerent.

Fear like he'd never felt before gripped the Gerent, and that was saying something, since Malbent lived in an almost perpetual state of fear when in the presence of Vicar. Staring up into the almost face of this giant beast as it approached, Jefferson Malbent almost relieved himself right then and there.

Grabbing Malbent by the throat, the Guardian lifted him from his feet and held him in the air, legs kicking and face tomato red, as his fingers scratched at the Guardian's arm.

Unable to breathe, Malbent thought his lungs had tasted their final gulp of air, as darkness began to crowd in from his peripheral. His head felt as if it would pop like an overblown balloon. Unable to scream, he made small mewling noises.

Suddenly, the Guardian released him, and the Gerent dropped to the ground like a sack, crumpled, limp.

Gasping for air, his chest heaved, each breath burning in the sweetest way. He was alive, when only moments ago he had thought that he'd taken his last breath.

"Get up," Vicar commanded. "You still have much to do. Take this as a warning. I will not accept failure again. I'm certain you understand the consequences if you do."

Vicar rose to his feet and stood over the cowering Gerent Jefferson Malbent, who scrabbled back against the wall.

"Rise, I said. We have a war to fight, and you need to get yourself together. You *are* the face of Elan. You must stand tall and look strong if the people are to stand behind you." Vicar turned to his Guardian. "In the meantime, we have our own work to do."

Finally mustering the strength, Malbent stood and found his footing on quaking legs. The beast was still towering over him, next to Vicar.

Then, they turned and headed down the stairs, into the underground passage.

19

JASON

Expecting a return to the place where I'd gotten my weapons, I was surprised when we ended up on the outskirts of Elan at a guard shack in front of a razor-wire topped fence. The guard came out and looked at each of our five faces, then turning to Agent Reece as she displayed her credentials, he asked, "What is this?"

"That's none of your business," she replied. "External Security doesn't answer to you. Now, open the gate."

He went back into the shack, and a few seconds later, the gate rattled back on a squeaky wheel, allowing us entrance to the facility.

As we walked toward the low slung, industrial white building, Reece said, "The freezer is in the back and it's under constant guard. That's where the antivirals will be, along with a bunch of other really nasty bugs. So, be careful not to get the wrong thing."

"You're not coming?" Sanjay asked.

"I'm already here. But if anything happens to any one of us, then the others know where to go," Reece said as we reached the door.

A guard at the desk right inside the door looked up as we entered, and Agent Reece flashed her credentials once again, and he waved us in with an odd look on his face.

The inside was nothing special, but clean in an industrial way, its white tiled floor gleaming under the harsh overhead lighting.

Turning down a corridor, its walls lined with nondescript wood doors, I thought about how easy this had all been. Agent Reece showing up out of nowhere with a group of unidentified companions couldn't be a common occurrence. Trying to convince myself that I was just being paranoid, I pushed my concern to the side and followed her down the hallway.

But that itchy feeling wouldn't go away.

Making a turn into another corridor, we ran right into a team of guards, each man pointing a Scythe in our direction.

"Freeze where you are," said a man in the middle at the front of the pack. Big and burly, he looked like he spent a lot of time in the gym.

If we turned and ran, we'd just be shot on the back. If this was the end, I wanted to go facing my killer.

"Now would be a perfect time for that mind control thing," Reece said, standing beside me.

Remembering what she'd said earlier, I attempted to relax. I could feel the buzzing current, but it wasn't as strong as I felt it should have been. Concentrating, I tried urging the guards to lower their weapons, but nothing happened. We just continued our standoff as the seconds ticked by at a syrupy pace.

Tightening his hand around the grip of his weapon, one guard to the right fired his Scythe. The hallway being as quiet as a vacuum, I heard the soft *pfft* of the Scythe as it discharged.

Brit laced her fingers through mine, giving my hand a tight squeeze. The buzz kicked into high gear at her touch. Time slowed even further. I could see the cartridge as it cut through the air, the currents flowing around the projectile, creating little swirls as it passed.

Holding my free hand out in defense, I felt the energy converge in my defending hand. The cartridge stopped mid-flight, froze for a second, then dropped straight down to the floor.

Which must have put the entire team of guards on edge, because they all fired, simultaneously, releasing a chorus of *pffts* as their cartridges fired.

This time, as the energy converged in my hand, I concentrated, focusing the energy not only at the cartridges, but at the guards beyond. The corridor walls looked as if they had warped for a second, the overhead lighting dimmed. Brit clutched my hand tighter.

The cartridges not only stopped, but were blown backward, as were the guards, falling into each other then to the floor.

Tristan and Sanjay rushed forward to collect their weapons, a small arsenal of Scythes.

Agent Reece was staring at me. "Your eyes," she exclaimed. "Oh, my God. I knew, but to actually see it. It's... The stories are true.

More guards could be on their way, and the freezer is just around the next corner. We need to hurry."

Done collecting the weapons, Sanjay and Tristan stood, and we all rounded the next corner. Which turned out to be just like all the others in this building.

"Last door on the right," Reece said.

But before we could make it, a door on the left side of the hallway opened and a man stepped out.

I knew this face.

The guy from the woods that had been kicking my ass.

"What's up, cousin," he said as he faced me. To Agent Reece, "You know this is treason, right?"

Squeezing Brit's hand, I said, "Go. Get the cure. It's the one with the yellow top."

Then I rushed Nate, wrapping my arms around his waist and slamming him into the wall.

Dropping an elbow onto my back, he pushed me off and threw a front kick to my chest.

Brit and Agent Reece took advantage of my distraction, making it to the door only to discover that it was locked.

Crashing into the wall, the wind was knocked out of me and I almost crumpled to the floor.

Moving faster than anyone I'd ever seen, he was on top of me, throwing a succession of lefts and rights, and all I could do was get my hands up to deflect as many blows as possible.

A loud boom shook the hall as Tristan kicked the locked door that separated us from the cure. Solid and study, the lock held and Tristan kicked it again.

And again.

And again.

Shifting my weight and spinning away from Nate's barrage, I gave a heavy hook to his ribs and he slid a few feet back.

Opening with a bang, the door, at long last, found freedom from its locking mechanism, and everyone rushed into the lab, leaving Nate and me in the corridor, alone.

Pressing my advantage from the rib shot, I made to throw at his face, but he drew a short sword. Not having the time to draw the Scythe in defense, I attempted to use my force to stop his strike.

Remembering to relax while simultaneously focusing my energy, I tried to control Nate's sword hand.

And it worked. Sort of.

Expecting the same reaction I'd gotten with the guards, I was surprised when he pushed back with equal force. We stood there, equal in strength, his blade and my force deadlocked in a stalemate of wills.

"Help me, Nate. Help me get the cure," I said.

Then, I was bowled over. Out of nowhere. Completely unexpected. One moment I'd been standing there, the next I was crashing to the floor.

Rolling onto my back, I looked up into the face of a monster. Well, not quite a face, but the impression of a face.

The beast was huge.

Rolling out of the way just as he tried to stomp down on my head, I regained my footing and stood up.

On my feet he looked even larger.

What the fuck!

This thing had to be over seven feet tall and as chiseled as the Incredible Hulk.

As he swung a cinder block of a hand at my face, I ducked and side-stepped, circling around it. Delivering a blow that did absolutely nothing, I took a step back and tried using my force to no avail.

"If anyone is going to kill you, it's gonna be me," Nate said and joined the fight, swinging his sword, digging into the flesh of its arm.

Turning toward Nate, the beast backhanded him with the sword still lodged in its arm.

Nate went flying, dropping to the floor with a crash and skidded across its shiny surface.

I delivered a kick to its knee, then threw a right to its semi face, and it returned its attention to yours truly.

Striking my chest, the thing sent me flying as well, then stalked toward me to finish the job.

Sanjay came out of the door and, seeing the beast, drew a Scythe and fired cartridge after cartridge, but the monster was unaffected and kept coming toward me.

The ground began to shake, and the building rattled noisily. I thought we must have been having an earthquake, having never experienced one.

Brit, Reece, and Tristan ran out of the door and, upon seeing the monster, froze in their steps.

The rattling of the building grew in intensity as it got louder.

Falling from above, a chunk of the ceiling came down on top of the beast, crushing it to the floor.

Looking beyond the wreckage, I saw Nate standing there, arms raised as he worked to bring the building down with his force.

"Nate," I yelled. "You don't have to do this!"

But, he continued, eyes glowing.

"Nate! Stop!"

Using my force, I sent him tumbling while he'd been focused on the building.

The ceiling started collapsing in earnest and Brit grabbed my arm, pulling me away just as a chunk of building fell onto Nate.

"Nate!" I called again as I was pulled away from the collapsing roof and into another corridor.

"Did you get it?" I asked Brit as we ran toward the exit.

Tapping her hand against a small bag that was slung across her shoulder, she said, "Right here."

20

JASON

After getting away from the lab, Reece still with us, we made it to the road leading to Tristan's community, where we parted ways with him.

"I have to get back to Nana," he said as we stood at the turnoff.

"Come to Gutenberg soon and find us," I said. "If you can't make it we'll see you when we head back this way."

We all gave him hugs, then he went on his way, soon disappearing down the road.

Making it to Gutenberg in good time, we first passed the oil rigs and saw a heavy presence of fighting men. One stopped us and we were asked to identify ourselves.

We did, and then I asked, "What's going on?"

"Another breakout. Have any of you been bitten?"

"We haven't even seen any dead," Reece said.

"Well, they're out there," the man said. "Few of them in there, too." He gestured toward the city wall.

After they allowed us to pass, we continued on until reaching Gutenberg's gate, which was closed. A man yelled down from the top of the wall, "What's your business here?"

"Word is going around that the virus is back," Reece said. "And we believe we have the cure."

"What are you? A bunch of kooks? Trying to sell us snake oil." He started to turn away.

"We're not trying to sell anything. We just robbed a lab and almost died to get it. We can help."

He must have believed her because the gate cranked open enough for them to pass through.

The streets were mostly empty except for a few people, and they were all armed.

Approaching a man with a bald head and a neat beard covering his face, I asked for directions to their medical facilities, and he pointed us toward the center of the city.

Traffic was nil, so we made it to the clinic fairly quickly. After passing through the door we saw that the interior was a frenzy. The waiting room was packed to capacity, with armed men standing around on the lookout for anyone turning.

Approaching the desk, Reece asked, "Who's in charge here?"

"Are you bitten?" the receptionist responded.

"No."

"Is anybody in your party bitten?"

"No," Reece repeated.

"Then why are you here?" The receptionist had a bit of fatigue and frustration in her voice.

"I need to talk-" Reece continued.

But I tuned her out, the entirety of my attention going to the woman walking around the corner, entering the waiting area wearing a white lab coat.

As her eyes scanned across my face, she stopped dead in her tracks and, after a second, a huge smile split her face.

Running up to me, she threw her arms around my neck, squeezing me tight as I stood there, arms limply hanging at my side.

Breaking away, she said, "Oh, my God. It's you! You're alright. I didn't know what happened to you."

"I was going to be executed for what you got me into!" I growled. "Then you just disappeared. I had no one to stand up for me."

The receptionist came from behind the desk and asked, "Princess Miranda, is everything alright?"

Princess?!

"Princess? What is she talking about?"

"That's why I left so quickly," she explained. "I couldn't have been caught in a place like that."

"I was defending you." Then, I remembered why we were here. "Look. We'll talk about this later. I'm here because we have the cure."

21

VICAR

The chains jingled, alerting Vicar to the fact that she'd finally awakened. He'd been reading a book, a uniquely interesting one on necromancy.

Candle light reflected from her eyes as she checked out her surroundings. Fear emanated from her in waves, although she tried to hide it.

She was brave.

But he had a remedy for that.

Silence is uncomfortable for most, so Vicar continued reading, ignoring her for the most part. He figured she would say something once she couldn't take it anymore.

He was right, but it had taken longer than expected.

"What do you want?" the woman spat, her voice full of venom.

Closing the book, Vicar said, "Good morning."

"Hmph," was all she offered in response.

"Not much for pleasantries, I see," Vicar said. "Ok then. I'll tell you why you're here. You're the most powerful witch within reasonable distance, and I need a spell cast that only a very powerful witch can perform. I have a need and you fit the bill perfectly."

"You won't get away with this," the woman hissed. "My coven will-"

Interrupting her, Vicar said, "Yes. The Coven of Lilith. You've been out so you obviously haven't heard. Your coven has been destroyed and your compound burned to the ground. There will be no rescue. There will be no escape. You will perform the spell I need, and maybe we can talk about keeping your life, after."

Walking over to the woman, he crouched before her, taking her chin between his thumb and finger.

"There's a spell," he began. "Allows a person to control the dead."

"I don't do necromancy," she interrupted.

"Oh, you do now."

"Never!"

"You're going to give me the power to control the dead." Standing, he went back to his chair.

"I won't!"

"I like a woman with resolve. Too bad I've already given myself to The One." Vicar turned his head. "Bring him in!"

A priest in black robes entered, dragging a young man by the arm. Face swollen with dried blood at the corners of his mouth, he'd obviously seen better days.

"Tristan!" the woman exclaimed as soon as she saw him.

Looking up, Tristan said, "Nana!" Trying to run to her, he was snatched back by the priest clutching his arm.

"As I said, perform this spell and maybe we'll talk about your life. But you have my word that this young man will walk out of here free and alive." Vicar gave the priest a nod and he left the room, dragging Tristan behind.

"Decisions. Decisions," Vicar teased. "Don't take too long,

though. These cells can be particularly dangerous places for young men of his age."

PART II

22

MATHOR

It's been said that greed darkens the hearts of men, sowing envy and self-centeredness, building a lack of regard for one's fellow man - and/or woman. Greed is an equal opportunity employer, ignorant of race or religion, country or creed, sex or handicap.

Greed welcomes all. It doesn't discriminate one bit as it works its jagged claws into the soul, refusing to let go. The object of said greed can pull blinders over one's eyes, allowing them to only see their desire fulfilled, while a cloud of oblivion obscures rational thinking and logic.

Mathor had been dreaming. Not the dreams that pull you into an alternate life while you sleep. No, these dreams were more conscious of thought. Dreams raised on a diet of crappy jobs and under-achievement. Dreams built on a foundation of disappointment and jealousy.

He wanted to live like a king. With an estate and a hundred slaves. With more food than he could possibly eat. With beautiful women at his beck and call.

Mathor was tired of being the slave, working for hours on end, only to return to his small, single room apartment. The cold, barren quarters only served as a toxin upon his soul, and instead of appreciating the fact that he was a survivor, he felt as if he'd survived the Z Wars for what... This? A small closet and servant's wages?

And now, after all the years of standing idly by, waiting on that one golden opportunity to be dropped in his lap, it was finally staring him smack dab in the kisser. All he had to do was take it, seize the day, carpe diem and all that.

"I'm tired," Mathor said to his friend as they walked into the clinic to begin their shifts as orderlies.

"Didn't get much sleep last night?" the friend questioned in response.

"Not that. I'm tired of this," he said, looking around the waiting room. "Look how we're living and we're not even getting hazard pay. Look how we've *been* living. When was the last time you were with a woman?"

Staring blankly back, his friend said nothing.

"You can't even remember, can you? That's exactly what I'm talking about." He lowered his voice. "But I have a plan."

"What plan?" his friend asked.

Bringing his voice down to a barely audible whisper, Mathor gave a brief run-down of what he'd planned.

"No," his friend said once he was finished. "We can't. What if we get caught?"

"We'll still be living miserable lives until they take our heads. But we won't get caught."

"I don't know..." Skepticism coated his voice like an oil slick.

"Don't tell me you're scared," Mathor said to his friend. "That's how they keep us from being too ambitious. Don't break the rules, you'll get in trouble. Who makes the rules? Did you have any say so when they did? Fuck them. Let's make our own rules!" Mathor's's voice was passionate, the gravity of his words starting to hit home.

"You sure about this?" his friend questioned.

"Does shit stink?" he fired back.

"Ok," his friend, and now co-conspirator replied. "I'm in. But if I lose my head I'm gonna kill you."

"Deal," Mathor said with an expectant smile beginning to form.

The door to an examination room opened and the two men paused, nervously waiting on a nurse to come out and walk past them before continuing on to their destination. Passing a few more closed doors, they turned a corner into an area never seen by patients, at least not those still in the land of the living.

Continuing past the closed break room door and a couple others, the duo found the door they were looking for and opened it.

Stainless steel drawers lined one side of the wall, but they flashed by, unnoticed, as the men made for the small freezer at the back of the room. Securing the freezer were a hasp and lock, which Mathor gave a brief tug before looking around the room.

A gleaming examination table caught his eye and Mathor noticed a pair of rib shears resting near the table's drain. Snatching them up, he rushed back to the freezer, jammed one of the handles into the lock and pulled. Then twisted. Grunting with effort, he gave it all he could.

Nothing.

Stepping away from the freezer, he released the shears and they clattered to the floor.

"You said this would be easy," his friend, worried, said aloud.

"Shut up." Frustrated and thinking, he didn't have time to coddle his friend.

Looking back down at the rib shears, Mathor plucked them up and began working the blade into the softer material of the freezer's door, hands flexing as the shears bit further into the door with each squeeze.

Finished cutting around the hasp, he opened the freezer to

the sound of the seal breaking and a rush of cold air. The freezer was empty, except for the single canister sitting right in the middle of the desolate, tundra-like atmosphere.

Pulling a small trash bag from beneath his belt, Mathor grabbed the canister and delicately placed it inside of the bag.

After stepping toward the freezer, his friend tried to restore the hasp to its former position as unobtrusively as possible, but the weight of the lock kept pulling it out of position, until finally, he threw his hands up in frustration and stalked off behind Mathor, who was carrying the trash bag toward the rear exit.

Outside, the morning sun was bright as the two men crossed the lot to the narrow street behind the clinic. The urge to take off at a run was increasingly present, but they fought it off, knowing it was better to stay cool and not draw attention.

"Where are we going to take it?" his friend asked.

"Out to the Western Badlands. We'll be showered with gold, I'm telling you. We'll probably end up in a bidding war for a weapon like this. The power to start the next apocalypse? Everybody's going to want to get their hands on this!"

"We can't just walk out of the front gate. There are guards along the road for miles. We'll never make it!"

"What's my name? You should already know that I have another way," Mathor boasted as he led his friend through the winding streets of Gutenberg.

Walking into the more downtrodden section, they approached a door and knocked before going inside. A group of people sat around the front room, the most notable of whom was an older woman with a head full of gray hair.

Mathor spoke to the woman, "Hey, Ruth! I need to talk to you."

Rising from her chair, she said, "Come on into the kitchen. We can talk there."

Following Ruth into the kitchen, they sat at a round table.

"I need to use your tunnel. My friend and I need to get out of the city undetected," Mathor said.

"My son always thought highly of you," Ruth responded.

"I miss him."

"You were one of the few people who tried to help him whenever he got into a bind. I've always told you that if you need anything you can come to me. When do you plan on coming back? The other end of the tunnel has to be opened from the inside, and if we don't know when you're coming back, you'll be stuck."

"This is a one way ticket. We won't be coming back," Mathor replied.

"Oh? Well, go get your friend, then," she said, standing.

Leading the two men into the basement, Ruth opened a panel in the floor, exposing a ladder that descended into a tunnel that had been used to smuggle petroleum, kerosene, and gas out for sale on the black market in gallon jugs. It angled deep into the earth, beneath the city's wall and into the forest beyond.

Before descending the ladder, Ruth grabbed him into an embrace and said, "You be careful out there. We're going to miss you."

"You should think about getting out of here," he responded. "There has to be more for us out there."

"My place is here. And I'm too old. Now, get out of here!"

Releasing the embrace, Mathor and his friend climbed the ladder down into the dark tunnel, expectations of a new life guiding their way.

23

JASON

"Move your body behind your swing," I instructed, my hardwood staff colliding with Brit's as we trained in the front room of a vacant storefront.

Working left to right, right to left, I rhythmically swung my staff in slow arcs, allowing her to block each strike like a metronome keeping beat to a song. Picking up the intensity, I came harder, faster. Brit kept up for a moment, but then, she began backpedaling to avoid my attack.

"Never move backward, only side to side. You don't want to take yourself out of range for your own attack, and it's also easier to stop your opponent's attack the closer you are to their body," I said.

Demonstrating, I poked and sliced, thrust and swung my staff at her so that she could see how hard it would be to stop the attack from this distance. Brit managed to stay just outside of range, but her reaction time had significantly slowed in response.

She lunged forward, surprising me, and released a frustrated growl. I was just able to turn my body as her staff stabbed at my belly.

"Good," I said. "But don't stop moving. Transition immediately into your next attack. A moving target is the hardest to hit, and a never ending attack is the hardest to avoid."

Determination set on her face, the drops of sweat falling from her forehead went unnoticed. She took a deep breath, then set her feet to rush forward again.

A sharp rap on the storefront window caused both of us to start, and I looked up to see a Royal Guard staring at us through the grime that had built up on the oversized pane.

After crossing to the door, I was greeted with a gruff, "Your immediate presence is required at the palace."

I turned around to grab my bag, which was sitting right inside the door.

"Your *immediate-*" he began again.

Holding my bag high so that he couldn't possibly miss it, I said, "Got it. Immediate. Let's go."

Chest heaving, Brit had one eyebrow raised in question as I looked back at her, but I just shrugged my shoulders in response.

I didn't have a clue.

It almost felt like I was in trouble. A distant memory came to mind from my first grade class. One of my friends had thrown a penny at me, and in response, I tossed it right back at him. Only, my timing had been horrible and the teacher, Mrs. Holden, turned around as the penny was leaving my hand to begin its arc through the air. Her voice froze me in place as she screamed my name and told me to foot it directly to the principal's office. My feet had been ball and chain heavy as I made my way down the empty, quiet halls.

That's exactly how I felt as I followed the Royal Guardsman down the street toward the looming palace which towered above, masquerading as a skyscraper.

Walking through the entrance, two guards nodded at their counterpart who guided me through the building and up to the tea room, where King Morgain sat in a plush chair, a carafe of coffee, sugar and cream on the dark, polished coffee table before him.

Sitting on a small sofa to the King's left, I couldn't help but feel uncomfortable beneath the weight of his silent stare. He said not a word for the next few minutes. Just sat there, fingers steepled beneath his chin, staring through me, I now realized.

Miranda stepped into the room and the air was immediately charged. Being the first time I'd seen her since the last time I'd seen her, which had been our first encounter since my stint as a condemned man, I was once again struck by her beauty. Even though I did feel like she was in some part responsible for my time on death row, which caused me to hold on to a lingering bit of anger.

The Princess was gorgeous.

And clever, I reminded myself. The memory of how she'd pulled me into a situation in which I'd had to kill someone was still fresh, and I'd do well to never forget it.

Taking a seat across from me on my sofa's twin, Princess Miranda's brown eyes met mine, then she brushed an errant lock of wild, curly hair behind her ear.

King Morgain stared at me as well, his eyes an obvious original to his daughter's copy. He was focused this time, not looking into the ether beyond me.

"Where is it?" The king's voice was thunder, authoritative. It was also directed at me.

But I didn't have the slightest clue about what he was speaking.

Raising an eyebrow, I asked, "What are we talking about here?"

"That damned virus you brought into my city! This is on you. Your responsibility!" King Morgain leaned forward, resting his elbows on his knees. "I don't need this shit. We're already working our asses off trying to save everyone as it is. I don't need another canister of this stuff getting loose within our walls."

Miranda sat back, crossing her legs in the process.

"I didn't have anything to do with it. You have my word," I told the king.

"Miranda," he said to his daughter. "Do you believe him?"

"I do," she replied, offering a slight nod.

"I don't think you had anything to do with this, Jason," the king said. "But, you *did* bring this mess into my city. You will retrieve this damned virus and bring it back to be stored in my personal vault until we find a way to safely destroy it."

Standing, I said, "Consider it done, Your Highness."

Just as I reached the door, King Morgain called out, "One more thing."

Turning around, I said, "Anything."

"Princess Miranda will be accompanying you."

24

NATE

Cresting the hill into the final stretch leading to the village of Noid, Nate's horse raced toward the idyllic setting of large, cabin style homes backed by a mist-covered lake.

A figure appeared on the road, causing Nate's horse to pull up onto its hind legs, almost throwing him from the saddle, although he managed to keep his mount beneath him. One moment, the road had been empty, a clear path into the village. But within the blink of an eye the man was just there, patiently waiting, as if he'd been standing there for the past hour, anticipating Nate's arrival.

Managing to keep the fearful mare dancing forward, he started to get a closer look at the man. Dressed in a simple white shirt and khaki pants, the man held his arms out at forty-five degrees.

Nate blinked his eyes and when he opened them, the man was twenty feet closer. That fast. He hadn't seen the man move, not even a step. One moment he was there, and the next he was here.

Unable to hold on this time, Nate was thrown to the ground

as his horse pulled up again. Gaining his feet, he dusted himself off and looked at the man.

"Welcome traveler," the man said, his black eyes absorbing light like twin black holes. His skin was gray. Not the gray of the majestic elephants, but the gray of flesh that's been starved of oxygen. The gray of decay and desiccation. "What's your business with the Noid, may I ask?"

Staring into the Noid's twin, dark pools that acted as eyes, Nate said, "I need passage to the underworld, and it's my understanding that you can help."

"You will die."

"Say, what?" Nate asked in response.

"You must shed the vessel of this world to enter another, and the only way to release your spirit is by death of the flesh." The darkness where his eyes should have been swam with a current, then reverted back to their original, placid state. "A man must also be judged. But you are no man. Indeed, you are not. You have grace, so you will make the crossing without facing judgement. That you're not entirely of this world means that you have access to other worlds. Only, you must find the doors. You have, indeed, found one such door, my new, nephilim friend. Still, you must die."

"Nate. My name is Nate."

"I've been called many things," the man said. "You may call me Berlek."

Nate asked, "You will be able to bring me back, right?"

"You must return to the door through which you entered or find another. So long as you find your way, your vessel will be waiting." Turning around, Berlek said, "Follow me."

Climbing onto his saddle, Nate followed Berlek as the man took off walking.

After a few steps, Berlek suddenly appeared ten feet further along. Walking again until Nate and his horse caught up, he then appeared another ten feet ahead. They continued in this manner until reaching the village, where Nate dismounted.

Walking into the center of the village, they came upon a group of people milling about. A young man approached and took the reins from Nate's hand, walking off with his horse.

"She'll be well taken care of," Berlek said.

People began coming up to the two men, and soon a crowd formed. Nate noticed that all of the people in the village had the same necrotic, gray skin. Their eyes were all deep, black pools, the very absence of light. And they each wore simple clothes similar to Berlek.

The crowd parted as they moved forward, then closed in behind. Nate's arrival seemed to cause quite the spectacle. The entire village had to be out here inspecting their most recent visitor. A couple of children ran up and threaded through Nate's legs like the eye of a needle. A few people reached out and touched him as they passed.

All of the attention made him slightly uncomfortable, especially considering Berlek had just told him that he would have to die. Was this his funeral procession? Did everyone come out for the excitement of his anticipated death?

Uncomfortable, Nate instinctively moved his hand toward his hip, reaching for his Scythe. Nothing there. Giving himself a thorough pat-down, he almost panicked. His head swiveled around as he searched the crowd.

What the fuck happened to my weapons?

The onyx eyes of the villagers revealed nothing. Berlek stared straight ahead. At least his head was facing forward, but a slight smile played on his lips. There was no telling what their eyes were actually looking at. No pupils to follow. Just twin lumps of coal that sometimes rippled with waves.

"They've never seen an angel before," Berlek said as they walked towards the lake.

Nate responded, "I'm not an angel."

"Ah, but your grace shines like a beacon for those with the ability to see. Noid have the sight. Your presence has stirred up quite the commotion."

"Where are my weapons?" Nate asked.

"You don't need them here."

"Answer my question."

"They are safe. Just like your horse. All of your belongings will be returned to you once you're back from the underworld. They're not necessary here, only a threat to my people." Berlek gestured toward a pit that had been dug in the sand of the lake's beach. "We will eat first, then you will begin your journey."

A fire roared from the pit, as Nate replaced the word 'journey' with 'death' in his mind. This was looking more like a funeral feast with every passing minute.

A noise from behind startled Nate, and at first he thought an infant was screaming. Turning, he saw blood pouring from the slit neck of a goat, its legs weak as it stumbled forward and fell to the earth. Two men hefted the goat onto the shoulders of another man who carried the animal off to the back of one of the cabins, out of sight.

"Where do you all come from?" Nate asked.

"We've always been here," Berlek replied.

"Right here? Even before the world ended? It's just that I've never seen anyone who... looks like you."

Berlek said, "The world didn't end. Here we stand."

"You know what I mean." Nate looked at him, annoyed.

"The world ending - as you put it - had a peculiar side effect. The curtain that conceals the worlds within this world was pulled back, revealing everything. Before, we wore legends that allowed us to move freely, and no one was ever the wiser. Only those with the sight were ever aware of our presence. When the change occurred..." Berlek spread his arms. "Legends no longer worked. The Council of Others met, but nobody had a clue."

"Others?" Nate questioned.

"There are many different peoples who inhabit this world, as well as others. Some look similar to you, such as my Noid. And there are others who look less like you."

Two men came around the cabin carrying the goat, which had been cleaned and secured to a spit. Hoisting it above the fire, they placed the ends of the spit onto Y shaped poles.

Four men approached the roasting goat, taking position at each of the four poles: north, east, south, and west. Red robes billowing in the wind, they raised their faces to the sky and sang what Nate assumed was a prayer. The tone was hopeful and thankful as their voices resonated over the surface of the lake.

Once the four men were done, a group of teenagers demanded everybody's attention as they started dancing to the rhythmic beat of a drum. Their dance was energetic as they stamped their feet to the beat while writhing about, colorful tassels pirouetting on their white dresses.

The drumbeat gained intensity as the crowd began to chant and clap their hands. The chant was infectious and Nate felt the urge to join in, but he didn't know the words yet and wasn't comfortable trying to say what he didn't know, but he did add the sharp sound of his own hands clapping together.

Standing before Nate, Berlek raised a thumb dripping with ochre paint to Nate's forehead, dragging a dark red stain down to the tip of his nose. Standing back, he inspected his artwork and issued a nod.

The group of dancers approached and pulled Nate into their performance. It didn't take long before he got the hang of it, and Nate joined in earnest. The entire ceremony was infectious and he could feel the spirit, so to speak. Endorphins and all of those other feel good chemicals were definitely flooding his system.

He'd even forgotten that this celebration was in anticipation of his upcoming passing.

A man cut through the crowd of dancers. His face was also painted with ochre, white, and yellow streaks. Short of stature, he was almost what people used to call a little person, but not quite. He couldn't have been an inch over five feet, but Nate registered his presence as if the man was of mammoth proportions. He had a presence, an aura that could fill a room. Or a crowded beach.

Walking directly up to Nate, the man held out a hand as if he were going to blow Nate a kiss. And blow the man did, but it was no kiss that blew in Nate's direction. A puff of white powder floated up, surrounding Nate's head.

At first, Nate was alarmed, but the powder found immediate access to his bloodstream through Nate's dark brown eyes. It was pulled deep into his lungs as Nate took his next breath. He could taste it in his mouth, the back of his throat.

The effects were fast coming on. Colors were super vibrant, almost glowing. There were two of everybody, and soon there were three of everybody. Shadows began creeping into his peripheral and Nate turned his head side to side searching for the source, but the shadows continued to creep ever more inward, inward until Nate could only see a pinprick of light.

Then, nothing.

25

NANA

The dimly lit corridor reeked of mildew as Nana's footsteps echoed lightly off the dark, stone walls. Small goosebumps prickled on the flesh of her thin arms as she crossed through a pool of wan light that spilled from one of the tiny bulbs spaced intermittently along the cool passageway.

Not knowing how long she could go unnoticed, Nana had planned on making this a short excursion. Picking up the pace, she was breathing heavily as she rounded a corner, but her destination was in sight.

"Tristan," she whispered, loudly, as she ran and crashed into the rust-spotted, steel bars of Tristan's cell.

Rising from a small cot and throwing a thin blanket to the side, he rushed to the bars as Nana's delicate hands came through, caressing his face.

"Oh, baby. How are you?" Her voice cracked with emotion.

Seeing Tristan locked in this dark, dank cell caused her stomach to turn in knots. Worry coated her heart as it drummed in her chest.

"I'm hungry." He could barely get the words out. "And thirsty."

The knots began to warm, a rising heat in her belly that intensified with every passing second.

"I'll bring you some food. I promise." Nana's hands squeezed Tristan's cheeks. "I don't have long. Vicar had some emergency and took most of the guards with him."

"You can't do what he wants," Tristan blurted.

"I won't let them hurt you." Her voice was a soothing whisper, a calm ocean breeze washing over fine grains of white sand. "Before Vicar's spell can work he must get milk from the Poppy of Paradise. This poppy only grows in one place."

"You can't help him, Nana. I don't care what they do to me," Tristan interrupted.

"Hush, boy. In the far reaches of the underworld in the Hambrathia region, there's a valley. One single valley. And these little prune looking poppies cover the entire valley floor. Like walking through a field of cow shit, I read in a journal a long, long time ago." She said the last with a chuckle.

Tristan stared blankly, not believing Nana would help someone like Vicar.

"This poppy," she continued, "also has another rumored purpose. It's supposed to be poisonous to angels."

Tristan's shoulders rose in frustration. "Vicar's not an angel! How does that help us?"

"Without Nate, Vicar only has his magic. Which is powerful, child. Let me tell you. But my magic is powerful too. And with Jason's help, Vicar doesn't stand a chance."

Hope sprang into Tristan's eyes. "How do we get this poppy?"

"We don't."

"Then-"

"We can't access the underworld. Or, at least I haven't found a way for mortals to make the passage and live." She paused for a second. "Nate's going."

Nana's heart jumped into overdrive as the soft echo of

distant footsteps caught her attention. A pair of voices, low and garbled, filtered through the oppressive, stale air.

Tristan's eyes widened in alarm. "They're going to catch you!"

Ignoring his panicked warning, Nana's eyes searched the corridor. The walls had been roughly blasted from the bedrock beneath the temple, leaving no closets, crevices, or niches for her to duck into. Looking back in the direction from which she came, from which she heard footsteps and voices of people she absolutely couldn't let catch her down here, she scanned up and down, left and right. Looking for anything, anything to offer even the smallest amount of cover.

"Nana." Tristan's voice bounced off the corridor walls. "You gotta go!"

"Hush, Tristan!" Nana's voice was a harsh whisper.

Finding nothing, she turned toward the other direction, which was a dead end about twenty yards down from Tristan's cell.

Nowhere to run.

A brief moment of panic caused Nana's heart to flutter uncontrollably as butterflies spread their silky wings throughout her stomach.

The footsteps grew louder.

They were getting closer.

With nowhere to go, Nana scanned the small expanse of corridor and noticed a small, wooden crate. Burned into the side of the crate was a single word.

Explosives.

The crate must have been used to store and transport the dynamite used to blast into the bedrock.

Walking over to the crate, Nana stood beside it, wrapping her hand around a small leather pouch that hung from her neck on a thin leather string.

The voices were so close that Nana could distinguish their words.

"... Really creeps me out. You ever look into his eyes? It's like there's nothing there. Absolutely nothing." The voice was gruff, deep, giving Nana the image of a bear with a man's face.

The second voice was slightly slurred, as if his tongue had been thoroughly thickened by wine. "How many times I gotta tell you to stop talking like that? If someone hears you..."

"Piss off! Nobody around to hear me but you. You gonna rat me-"

"Of course not!" the second voice slurred.

The crate was much too small to hide behind; even if Nana - with her petite frame - were to fold herself as compactly as possible, she would still be glaringly obvious as soon as the men rounded the corner.

As the footsteps and voices became more of an immediate threat, Nana's thumb massaged the leather pouch and her lips moved in an almost inaudible whisper.

The incantation - recited in a long forgotten, ancient language - started to take effect. Nana's visage shimmered between solid and translucent, real and in-between for a moment, before completely disappearing.

Tristan stood there, mouth hanging open as he stared at a second wooden crate, identical to the one that had already been sitting on the corridor floor.

The mirroring spell Nana used was intended to shield one from sight and wouldn't hold up under physical contact, so as long as the dynamic duo didn't get handsy she should be fine.

The two guards rounded the corner, their yellow cloaks hanging limply in the stagnant air.

At least they're not Vicar's red-cloaked personal guard.

Walking up to the bars of Tristan's cell, the men looked at each other.

"Looks like he seen a ghost." The gruff voice did indeed

belong to a bear of a man, barrel chested with tousled, blond hair.

The second guy was just as big, but his head and face were shaved smooth. "Maybe he snapped, Roy." The slur was still present. "Being stuck down here by yourself will drive anybody crazy."

"Hey, boy," Roy of the gruff voice called out to Tristan. "Look at me!"

Snap out of it, Tristan!

"Look at him," Roy said. "Mouth hanging open like he's trying to catch flies. Hey boy! You hungry or something?"

Eyes blinking, Tristan closed his mouth and met Roy's eye. "Don't call me boy."

Laughter from the two guards.

Nana's blood began to boil. Not only was Tristan being held in this shit-hole of a dungeon to bend her to Vicar's will, but he also had to deal with this ridicule as well!

Struggling to bring the fire burning inside down to a low simmer, Nana fought to maintain her spell and remain unseen. She had to. The guards discovering her would cause Vicar to keep her under even heavier guard. She wouldn't be able to do anything for Tristan.

"He's fine," said the bald guard. "We need to finish our rounds."

Roy turned to his comrade and offered a crisp salute. "Yes, sir, Mr. By-the-book. Look around. Nobody's here to care, Pete."

Head shaking, Pete turned back to the main corridor. "I'm finishing my rounds. You can do what you want. But you're the one can't look Vicar in the eyes."

Roy visibly shivered at the thought. "Fucking creeps me out man. I'm coming, I'm coming."

Tristan glanced over at the dual wooden crates as Pete and Roy rounded the corner, out of sight. When Nana didn't immediately materialize, he whispered, "Nana! Nana, they're gone."

Another minute went by before Nana's image began to solidify.

As she stepped up to the bars, Tristan said, "That was so lit! How'd you do that?"

"I gotta get back. Be strong, baby. Vicar's days are numbered, but I need you to stay strong. Okay?" Her hands went to Tristan's face again. "Okay?"

"Yes, Nana."

With a final squeeze of Tristan's cheeks, she rushed off to the corner and peeked around before quietly making her way back to her quarters.

26

JASON

The mid-day sun was high and bright as Miranda and I walked the streets of Gutenberg in the direction of the clinic where the theft had occurred.

After the King's summons I had been somewhat irritated so I went to my small, one room apartment to shower, hoping my irritation would wash away along with the dried sweat and grime from this morning's workout.

I looked over at Miranda walking at my side and felt the tightness in my gut reappear. Two of the Princess's guardsmen followed a couple steps behind and Crush led the way as we wound down the smooth curves of a surprisingly busy street. Foot traffic darted back and forth from the row of busy shops to the crowded sidewalk as a few cars zipped down the meandering road.

Thinking back to my childhood before the pandemic hit I was reminded of how similar Gutenberg was to the way things used to be. I guess it inspired hope, but to me it just read false. Everyone was going about their lives like the Z Wars never happened, like people weren't showing up in the ER daily with fresh bites.

And if the virus made it outside of the city...

But that wasn't the source of my irritation. Miranda was. The thought of working with the woman who had set me up and left me for dead caused acid to burn holes in the lining of my stomach. How could I trust her when all she had shown me was how selfish she was?

"So you're just going to give me the silent treatment?" Miranda's voice was dark chocolate. Smooth and rich. "We're going to be spending a lot of time together until we find this virus of yours. Hopefully we find it sooner rather than later. But until we do we're pretty much joined at the hip. And no woman wants to be joined to a sulking man."

"Your team did a good job of getting the cure out." I wasn't sulking. "It's almost like things are back to normal. I mean, look at all these people."

"They couldn't wait for the restrictions to be lifted. I think most of them didn't really believe it was happening all over again." She tucked a wild curl behind her ear. "But we're still having some people come in with bites."

"Not to mention this missing canister." Sure, I didn't trust her. And I was feeling some kind of way about our brief past. But I wasn't going to act immature about it. We had to work together and it just is what it is. "What do you know of the guys who stole it?"

"Nothing. I didn't know either one of them."

"Oh. Since I saw you at the clinic I just assumed-"

"So don't assume things." Miranda's eyes bored into mine.

A little girl with bright blue eyes under a mop of brown hair ran up to us as her mother, tall and thin with the same blue eyes and brown hair, called after her, "Leigh! Leigh! Get back here!"

Ignoring her mom, Leigh issued a high pitch call of her own. "Princess! Princess Miranda!"

Our small coterie turned at the voices and all three guards

tensed at the disturbance until Crush, noticing that it was a little girl, allowed a blindingly white smile to break out of a face that was midnight. "Relax. It's just one of the Princess's fangirls."

Miranda put on a big smile as she squatted before the girl. "Hi, pretty. What's your name?"

Leigh nervously kicked her toe as she gave her name. "Leigh."

"Such a pretty name for a pretty little girl." Miranda brushed the girl's hair from her forehead with a thumb. "Do you want to be a princess one day?"

Leigh nodded as her mother caught up. "Oh my god. I'm so sorry. I apologize. She can be such a handful at times."

"It's absolutely okay. You have a beautiful daughter." Miranda stood and extended her hand. "I'm Miranda."

The woman gave an awkward bow before taking Miranda's hand. "Thank you, I'm Lynn. It's such an honor to meet you."

Lynn put an arm around her daughter's shoulder.

Miranda's teeth were straight and white as she gave Lynn a wide smile. "The pleasure is mine."

Miranda had a beautiful smile.

Lynn and Leigh turned and walked away as we stood there taking in the scene. The shops had been repurposed from an old shopping center that had sustained minimal damage during the Z Wars. Most of the buildings left standing were in need of major repairs, so finding an entire shopping center that was capable of conducting business was a lucky thing indeed.

"She's a cute kid," Crush said.

Miranda started off down the sidewalk, brushing past Crush. "The clinic is right around the corner. Let's get this over with."

27

NATE

Consciousness came slowly. He could hear no sound, see no light. But he was aware of awareness. There was no physical sensation either. Nate tried wiggling his toes but was unsure if he had accomplished his goal. This is what he would have imagined a sensory deprivation tank to feel like.

Sounds started to creep in. The steady beat of drums at first, soon followed by incomprehensible voices.

Everything started to come back to Nate and his heart beat rapidly with panic thinking of the goat roasting above the fire. Would he be next? Was this the beginning of some savage, torturous, cannibalistic ceremony? Well, technically, it wouldn't be cannibalism because the Noid were an entirely different species altogether. But still...

The voices came in more clearly with each passing minute, like someone was adjusting the tuner of an analog radio, trying to get the frequency perfect and get rid of the static.

Nate's brain struggled against the paralysis. He struggled to wiggle his toes, bend a knee, shrug his shoulders, flip the Noid the bird. Anything.

But nothing.

What the fuck!

Pinpricks of light appeared in his vision, blindingly bright even though Nate wasn't sure his eyes were even open. The searing luminosity burned his corneas, and Nate tried to close his eyes against the acute brilliance.

This wasn't what he'd signed up for. To be paralyzed, tortured, and eaten by some unknown species of people? Not at all.

Nate's vision cleared and he stared up at Berlek's decaying face, into his tenebrous eyes.

Berlek said, "You are now ready for your journey. Safe travels, my new friend."

Nate became aware of sensation on his skin, as if Berlek's words had flipped a switch and ignited his nerve endings. He was floating, gently bobbing on top of the water, no longer on the beach.

I can't swim!

Nate frantically kicked his legs and flapped his arms in an attempt to stay afloat. But it was of no use. The water began rising, covering his mouth. Rivulets streamed into his nostrils as Nate shook his head and blew air through his nose in a futile attempt to keep the water out, but soon he felt it at the back of his throat.

Fighting to keep the water from entering his lungs, Nate clutched at his throat with hands that couldn't offer any real aid. They just clutched and clawed as he struggled to not take a breath.

But he had to. His body couldn't resist any longer. That ancient part of his brain that controlled such functions would not be denied.

Nate inhaled.

The cool lake water burned as if it came from the pit of hell itself when it entered his lungs.

A dizzying array of color entered Nate's field of vision.

Yellows, blues, greens, and reds all swirled in a funkadelic kaleidoscope as he sank beneath the calm waves of the lake.

Talk about the fucking rabbit hole...

The colors began to dim, their luminosity dampened as if he were getting farther away from light in general. Farther away from life.

Deeper into darkness.

Everything went black and Nate wondered if he had died. Was this purgatory? He could still feel the water's cool embrace upon his skin. Do the dead still feel?

The firm embrace of a strong current tugged at his body, twisting him one way then another. There was no use trying to fight the current, it was just too strong. All Nate could do was... nothing. Just go with it.

Breaching the surface, Nate's lungs screamed for oxygen, but settled for a coughing fit, expelling all the water he'd inhaled.

Looking around Nate saw darkness, but this wasn't the darkness of death. This was more of a gloom, as if clouds were filtering the light of the moon and stars. There wasn't even a reflection to be seen on the water's surface.

Nate's head plunged beneath the water and he remembered that he couldn't swim. Arms flailing, he slapped at the water, but it was useless. He began sinking as if his pockets were filled with boulders.

A firm grip clamped around Nate's wrist and he was yanked to the surface. A moment later a pair of hands grabbed him beneath his arms and Nate felt the hard edge of a wooden plank dig into his flesh as he was hauled onto a boat.

Nate stared up into a man's face. A man. Pale, extremely pale, he looked to be in his early thirties with straggly blond hair, a blond beard, and eyes of pallid, blue ice. "You're not Berlek."

"What's a Berlek?" the man questioned.

"Noid. What are you?"

He laughed heartily. "I'm a man."

Taking a moment, Nate looked over the man's tattered, reddish brown pants and tan shirt to his hand, where a long pole extended into the water below. "I'm Nate. What do they call you?"

"Charon." His voice was deep and rumbled throughout Nate's body.

Looking around, Nate tried to make out any kind of shapes or formations that would help him get his bearings. "Where am I?"

"This, young traveler, is the river Styx."

"You're not that much older than me."

Charon was silent as he dug the pole into the silt of the river's bottom, propelling the boat forward. "Looks can be deceiving. I've been around long enough to witness empires and kingdoms rise and fall. I've witnessed men worshipped as gods, and more gods than you can possibly imagine lord over the souls of men. You've lived but a day compared to me."

Chewing that over for a minute, Nate stood on wobbly sea legs, rocking the small, weathered boat.

"Careful." Charon grabbed Nate's arm, stabilizing him. "Angels and water don't mix."

Again with the angel stuff. "I'm not an angel."

"If you plan on living for any length of time you must truly know yourself. Your strengths as well as your weaknesses. You must know *what* you truly are and you are most definitely an angel, or at least part angel. A nephilim. And nephilim don't swim. Why do you think the earth flooded for forty days?"

Nate shrugged. "Yeah, I'm more free spirit than Bible thumper."

"To kill the nephilim," Charon continued. "Never forget that. It may serve you well someday."

"Well, thanks for the advice. I'll make sure to keep that in mind next time I'm in the shower." Dark outlines began to take shape as Nate looked out over the bow of the small craft. "Shore's coming up."

Charon said nothing, just kept digging his pole into the river bottom, propelling them forward.

As they moved closer to shore Nate noticed the long, gnarled branches of the strangest looking weeping willow trees he'd ever seen. The branches hung almost to the ground and reminded him of an old man's arthritic knuckles, knotted and twisted as they were.

The bottom of the boat hit solid land with the hollow scrape as Nate looked out to a narrow beach of dark sand. Leaping from the boat, he felt a sense of relief. Solid ground was beneath his feet. "How do I get to Hambrathia?"

Charon was already ten feet away from the shore. "My duty has been completed. May you fare well in the Whispering Wood."

Nate watched as Charon's silhouette disappeared into the dusk, then turned toward the tree line. As he approached, tension started to build in his body and his stomach tightened with nerves. The pace of his heartbeat picked up. His hands became slick with sweat. This wasn't something he was used to or could put his finger on, and he didn't quite understand it.

28

JASON

The clinic was fairly empty, and fortunately there weren't any bite victims awaiting treatment when we entered. A woman sat behind the desk, curvy with short blonde hair, tight eyes, and a rosy complexion. She flashed a big smile at Miranda as we entered and approached the desk.

The woman stood. "Princess Miranda, as always it's an honor. What can I do for you?"

"Tell me about the guy who stole the virus, Emily."

"Guys. There were two of them." She fell back into her seat. "Mathor and Ernie. Both of them have been janitors here for at least a couple years. They were friends and friendly enough with all of the staff."

I asked, "Has anyone been by their homes?"

Emily looked toward Miranda, who nodded. "Apartments. Living quarters really. I stopped by both of their places person-ally after my shift on the day the virus was stolen, but no one was at either place."

"Will you show us where it was stolen from?"

Miranda gave Emily another nod. "Yes, show us."

Emily came from around the desk. Crush and the other two

guards followed behind me and Miranda as she led us to the back of the clinic.

We entered a morgue, so to speak. Drawers that were used to hold and keep corpses frozen lined one wall, but we continued past them to a freezer with the door hanging ajar. It looked as if someone had taken a ragged bite out of the door where the lock was supposed to secure the hasp; only the insulation was still intact. On the jamb was a sturdy padlock connected to the hasp and latch with the cutout from the door framing the hasp like a dingy, white halo.

"What's the point of using a steel lock if they can just cut around it?" Miranda wondered aloud.

I had been thinking the exact same thing. "What did they use to cut it?"

Emily nodded toward a stainless steel examination table, on top of which rested a pair of small, odd looking bolt cutters. Only they didn't seem quite as sturdy. "Rib shears."

Picking them up, I imagined myself cutting through the material of the freezer door and around the hasp. Imagined squeezing the rib shears, my hand flexing with enough tension to clip through the aluminum exterior.

Seemed easy enough.

"We need to go have a look at their quarters," I said.

Leaving Emily at the clinic, the five of us took to the streets again. A half hour had elapsed before we came upon an old motel that had been converted into an apartment building. Both Mathor and Ernie called this repurposed temporary living establishment home, although they lived on different sides of the single level, U-shaped structure.

We approached Ernie's place first and as I went to turn the knob on the weathered, hollow door, Crush spoke up. "Allow me. Never know what's on the other side."

"I'll be alright," I responded and gave the knob a twist.

Nothing. It was locked.

After taking a step back I raised a foot and crashed it into the door, right next to the knob. With a hollow crack, a hole opened up in the weak wood and my foot went clean through up to my knee.

Laughter erupted behind me. A deep, booming laugh, unadulterated in its amusement.

Jagged pieces of wood bit into the back of my knee causing a sharp, pinching pain, and as I pulled my leg back through I could feel the woods scraping down my calf until my leg thinned enough to have a little wiggle room.

Crush was cracking up, and as I looked back at him, he said, "Told you."

Ignoring him, I put my hand through the dark hole I'd just created, avoiding the ragged edges, and unlocked the door from the inside.

The room was pretty much everything you would expect from a small motel. There was a full size bed, table, two chairs, and a tv. A small convection oven/cooktop combination was the only thing that separated this room from its former motel grandeur.

But other than that it was neat. And sparse. A neatly folded stack of clothes on one of the chairs was the only thing that could be considered as clutter.

Miranda sat on the bed and opened the nightstand drawer to rifle through it. "There's nothing here."

We left, pulling the door up as much as possible, and a minute later I kicked in the door to Mathor's room. This time the door swung right open.

This room was a mirror image of the first, with one major difference: the place was a mess. The table was a hodgepodge of old magazines, loose magazine pages, and random scraps of paper. The bed was unmade. Dirty bowls and cups were set at random places. Clothes and shoes were scattered about the floor. Dried and burnt food clung to the small cooktop.

My skin crawled. I wanted to take another shower.

Once the pandemic started, the world experienced a technological sunset. There was no media, electrical grids shut down, and everything went black. Electronics soon died. I remember finding books in abandoned houses, trashed libraries, and sometimes in debris scattered alongside the road. I read as I hid from other people, both living and dead. I read as I sat in my cell waiting to be executed. Oddly enough, I read an abundance of books about forensic psychologists. Must have been a popular topic at some point of time. But in this moment, I wondered what those psychologists would have to say about this room.

Women in alluring poses stared back at us from the wall where he had cut the centerfolds from old pornographic mags and taped them across the walls. Images of firearms and knives also dotted the walls. A cross that had been turned upside down hung above the head of the bed.

Miranda, Crush, and I spread out around the cramped space to rifle through the mess as the other two guards took up positions right outside the door. I got the sense I was wading through shallow water as I kicked through the clothes and other debris on the floor.

Entering the bathroom at the back of the room, I studied a toilet that looked as if it was waiting to give me some kind of horrible butt-borne disease. The mirror above the sink was dirty and it was hard to make out the fine details of my face as I stared at my reflection.

The shower, though... That was spotless. Pristine even. Not even a smudge of soap scum could be seen.

Too bad it smelled like the toilet looked.

"Hey! Check this out." Crush's voice filtered through the open bathroom door.

As I stepped out of the OCD inducing waste disposal facility, I caught sight of Crush standing next to the table with a magazine in his hand.

"It's an old Robb Report. My man has expensive tastes." He held the cover up for Miranda and me to see.

Miranda looked thoughtful. "Maybe he intends to sell it and not release it. That's a relief, to some extent."

"But who would he sell it to?" I stepped around the bed and stood next to Miranda.

"No one here, I'm certain." Miranda seemed to study my face. "They have what's practically a weapon of mass destruction. My father is the only person in Gutenberg capable of buying such a weapon but he only wants to see it destroyed."

"Back to Elan, then." I said it, but I wasn't so sure.

"No," Miranda said. "They want what we have. Elan is attacking us because we have resources they can't afford."

"I would head west." Crush piped up.

"Yes." Miranda laughed, a clever look in her eyes. "The west abounds with tales of gold and riches. Exotic women and rivers of wine."

Crush just might have been onto something. Depending on how ambitious and clever these guys were they could use the weapon to start their own little kingdom. And what better place to do that than out west? Even if they were only looking for a bag of gold the best way to go would be west.

"I'm with Crush," I said. "West is the way to go with something that dangerous. It's going to take a sociopath to buy a fucking weaponized Z virus and I bet we'll find a lot of them in the western badlands. The average person won't want to be within a ten mile radius of that damn virus."

"We'll head west." Miranda brushed past me and out the door and motioned to the two guards outside. "Grab your things. And, Crush, get us the five best horses in the city. We'll meet at the city gates in an hour."

29

NATE

After traversing the sandy beach, Nate stepped beyond the tree line, into the encapsulating darkness that clung to the ground beneath the dangling, overhead canopy. After a couple steps, a voice behind him whispered, "You let him kill her."

Turning around, Nate looked behind him and saw no one. Only the dense overhang of knotted tree limbs as they stretched their arthritic bones toward the ground. The beach was nowhere to be seen.

"Who's there?" he called out.

The only response was silence and the soft rustling of leaves as they brushed against one another.

"You let him do it and you didn't kill him."

He was taken back to when he was twelve years old. A couple years before the pandemic and the Z Wars. His dad had died a few years earlier, when he was nine. After his father's death things had gotten rough; money was slim. Nate's mother got addicted to drugs and in her necessity for money and to maintain that high she allowed drug dealers to use her house to conduct their business.

One morning Nate was awoken by the sound of loud voices in the living room. After climbing from his bed and walking out of his door he crept down the hallway to the end where he could peek around the corner, into the living room.

Nate studied his mom as she yelled back at the man. She was a shell of her former self. The years had taken their toll. She had taken his father's death really hard and it showed.

"I didn't do it!" she screamed.

"Bitch, who the fuck else took it? Casper the friendly fucking ghost?" The man was the latest hustler to use their small, rented house as a drug storefront. Average height with golden skin and long, curly hair, he was an imposing figure across from his vertically challenged mom.

"It wasn't me. Why would I steal from you, Dre?" she pleaded.

"My money, my dope... All gone!" Dre continued.

"I promise you baby, it wasn't me!"

"There's nobody. Else. Here!" Dre's hand went to the back of his waist and came out with a gun. He raised it to her stomach.

The crisp boom of the bullet leaving the chamber propelled Nate into motion and he spun around the corner.

Catching the movement, Nate's mom caught his eye and shook her head: no.

Nate stopped, confused. Concern for his mom pulling him in one direction and obedience to her instruction pulling him in another.

Falling to her knees, there was no sound but her lips were moving.

Nate read her lips. She was telling him to run.

Speeding back to his room, Nate entered and softly shut the door. His heart raced faster than any NASCAR had ever gone. His hands were slick and a droplet of sweat trailed from his underarm down the side of his chest.

After kicking on a pair of jeans and some shoes, Nate went to his bedroom window and opened it. After climbing out of the window and down to the ground, he ran. Ran down the street. Just ran.

Nate never looked back.

A piercing scream escaped his lungs and Nate fell to his knees just as his mother had done that day.

He sat there, air entering and exiting his lungs in gulps. Tears streamed down his face. His chin hung to his chest.

He should have done something that day. Anything. Screamed before the guy had a chance to pull his gun. Ran and tackled him. Kicked him between the legs.

Anything.

But he stood there, frozen like a deer in headlights. And then he ran.

He had never told anyone about that day. The sight of his mother's death had remained a closely held secret. Bottled up in the core of his emotions and buried beneath a beach of memories, each one a grain of sand ensuring that the guilt-ridden recollection would never resurface.

In the time since, he'd done a lot of bad things to guarantee that his nightmares consisted of even worse atrocities. But trust and believe that was a hard one to beat.

Where the fuck did that come from?

"You let her die. *You* did." The whispering voice had a slithery quality to it and he was reminded of a snake from some long forgotten animated film.

He needed a drink. A whole fucking bottle. And enough weed to knock him into a dreamless oblivion.

That had been Nate's respite for a while after his mother's death. He was a twelve-year-old addict, stealing everything he could in order to not think about his mom. But somewhere along the way he found his strength and ended up running a teenaged crew of thieves.

He needed that strength now. He needed to get up. He knew why he was here. His true motive. Sure, he needed that damn poppy, but it was just one piece in a bigger play.

Nate was well aware of his power, his strength, his speed.

He should have been the one giving orders, not taking them. There wasn't a man alive who could challenge him.

At least, until he ran into Jason.

Anger swelled in his chest as he thought about Jason, giving him the strength to rise to his feet. He didn't let that damn monster kill Jason because he wanted to be the one to kill Jason. And in order to kill Jason he had to get back to his feet and get on with it.

30

JASON

After packing my sleeping bag, a knife, a cooking pan, a few changes of clothes, and a kerosene stove for when firewood would be unavailable, I grabbed my e-spear, Scythe, and machete then set out to meet the others at the city's gate. Miranda and her three guards stood before the looming gate, and I noticed that she held the reins to a mount that was carrying a tent.

Fair enough. She would need her privacy.

Crush nodded toward a horse and I set my pack on the ground and rubbed my hand along its head and down its long nose. Then I secured my pack and climbed into the saddle.

The five of us rode out the gate and away from the city.

As we made it further away from Gutenberg the wild countryside sprang to life in a burst of color, and I was once again reminded of how beautiful the world was. Things as common as a blade of grass or a leaf from a tree, things we often take for granted, were the things that I was certain I would never see again. Now their vibrance was something that I couldn't help but appreciate.

Crush, as usual, rode in the front, followed by Miranda and

me with the other two guards trailing behind. It had been a quiet ride so far, but I was used to silence and solitude. Most people weren't comfortable in silence, but the years I had spent waiting to be executed gave me a certain appreciation for it.

"You can talk about it, you know." Miranda wore black boots, jeans that were tattered by either wear or for fashion purposes, and a long sleeve sweater that fit her body perfectly.

"Um... Talk about what?" She could have been talking about anything, but I had the niggling feeling that she was referring to our brief past history.

"Your time as a condemned man. That couldn't have been easy and talking about it might relieve some of the weight on your chest."

A soft breeze kicked up as she spoke, bringing with it the scents of sweet flowers with an undertone of something putrid. Maybe some predator had made a kill and we were nearing it. Maybe the virus has spread outside of the city and the dead were close by.

"There's nothing to talk about. It was five years of monotony, nothingness." I may have said it more sharply than intended.

"That's exactly what I'm talking about. Humans weren't designed for solitude. We're social creatures. We're meant to interact, and socialize, and be intimate. We're designed to crave the touch of another, or a hug. Even a kiss. You spent years without any of that." She paused. "What about sex? Oh, I couldn't imagine!"

I didn't want to talk about it, especially not with her. She hadn't been concerned when she disappeared and left me to face all of that by myself. She hadn't been concerned the entire time I was sitting there waiting to die. So why all the concern now? "There's a community not far from here called the Coven of Lilith."

"Coven?" Miranda interrupted. "As in witches?"

"We should stop and ask around about Mathor and Ernie. They're good people and I know they'll help if they can."

"So where is this 'Coven of Lilith'?" Thankfully, she let the previous topic of conversation go, although I was certain the subject would come up again on the long ride out west.

To be honest, I was surprised that she'd brought it up this soon.

After reaching the crossroads we turned toward the Coven of Lilith, traveling along the beaten up road. Too bad there weren't any maintenance crews to service the roads anymore. Without them, the roads were beginning to be reclaimed by nature. Weeds and grass were growing tall through the many cracks. Potholes were abundant. Even the horses had to be careful not to step wrong and break a leg.

The conveniences of civilization...

The sun was beginning to dip as we neared the coven. We were headed in a general northwest direction and the sun presented the perfect angle to see a haze in the sky.

"Forest fire?" one of the guards behind us questioned. This was the first time he'd spoken and I glanced back in the direction of the voice.

He was tall with long, thick, jet black hair. His dark eyes peered at the haze in the distance. He wore a black T-shirt and black cargo pants, the same as all of the other royal guards that I had seen in Gutenberg. The shiny surface of scarred flesh crossed his lips at a forty-five degree angle.

Crush responded, "Smells like it, Jael."

Jael didn't respond, instead reverting back to his previously silent self.

Soon enough, the Coven of Lilith appeared in the distance and the destruction was immediately apparent. Approaching the community, it was clear that the haze hanging in the air wasn't from the Coven, for the small community had been burned to the ground. Every single building was gone. All that remained were smoke-blackened rubble and ashes.

"Fuck!" I released a long curse.

"What happened?" Miranda asked.

"I don't know." The words softly slipped through my lips. "This wasn't an accident, though."

"Spread out," she called out to her guards. "See what you can find."

Crush, Jael, and the other guard rode off in different directions, leaving Miranda and me on what used to be the main street of the village.

Everything had been put to fire. Every home, building, and structure. This was the work of a large force.

Elan.

"Send one of your guards back to Gutenberg for Brit and Sanjay. They need to go to Elan and find out what happened to the Coven." It had to be Elan. This wasn't the work of slavers or bandits.

"No," Miranda's voice was steel. "We need every man for our trip west. What if this was because of a breakout? We'd lose a man for no reason. No, we can't do that."

We surveyed the scene in silence for a while. The clop-clop of horseshoes were the only sounds to be heard. No birds chirped. No bees buzzed. Only the rhythmic sound of horses walking down the street.

Twisted pipes jutted from the ashes, their tentacles alien against the lonely landscape. In the distance a scraggly dog looked in our direction then, realizing we were too far away to be of any harm, went back to rooting around in whatever had grabbed its attention.

There wasn't much to see, but there was one particular thing for which I had kept my eyes open; one thing I never saw.

"No bodies," I said.

"Nobody's what?" Her eyebrows were raised in question.

"This wasn't an outbreak. There are no bodies, no corpses. Nah. These people were taken and their village burned. Medieval style." I could tell that my words were beginning to penetrate.

Looking around, Miranda searched the ruins from a new perspective. Instead of looking for what was left, she started looking for what should have been there, but wasn't. Her face scrunched up in concentration, and in that moment I could see her as a child, a girl. A piece of that innocence still held root somewhere deep inside her.

Maybe I misjudged her, I thought. *There just may be hope for her selfish ass.*

"Shit. Okay." Her head shook in disbelief. "I'll send Robert. But you're right. I don't see any corpses or dead zombies. If Elan is really responsible for this..."

"Who else could it be, Miranda?" I asked. "Outside of Gutenberg, who has the kind of force that could do this? Elan, that's who."

"First the virus, now this." Her voice was soft and could barely be heard. "My father needs to prepare for war."

There was a sad anger in her eyes and I had the sudden urge to calm the turbulence.

Then I chided myself. *That's how you got in trouble last time.*

I couldn't understand why I felt compelled to come to this woman's aid. It wasn't because she was beautiful, even though she was. But I've known tons of beautiful women over the course of my life and none of them have had this effect on me.

Except Brit.

What I felt with Brit was something completely different.

This was... raw. Personal.

And I didn't appreciate it. I didn't want to feel compelled to help this woman. I didn't want to feel anything for this woman.

I didn't want to ever see her again.

I didn't *think* I'd ever see her again.

The sound of approaching horses roused me out of my thoughts. Turning around I spied Miranda's trio of guards. Robert and Jael were side by side, riding as if in formation with Crush in the lead. I hadn't paid any attention before, but now that I knew Robert's name I gave him the once-over. Slightly shorter than Jael, he had brown hair with blue eyes and a chiseled jawline.

"Nothing." Crush reported, looking at his princess.

"Robert." She stared past the commander of her personal guard. "You're going back to Gutenberg. I believe Elan to be responsible for this. Upon your arrival you will tell my father of this. And tell him to prepare for war. Then, you are to get Brit and Sanjay, and the three of you will ride to Elan. Learn everything you can."

"Tell Brit to find Tristan and Nana." I interrupted.

Miranda's eyes cut at me, but she spoke to Robert. "Go quickly! Tell my father."

Robert ran a hand through his mouse brown hair. "Yes, Princess!"

"It's getting late. We should set up camp somewhere for the night." I knew Brit and Sanjay would do everything they could to find Tristan and Nana.

31

NATE

His heart was racing and his lungs were sucking in bucketfuls of air as Nate emerged from the Whispering Woods onto a street in the middle of a city. The sky remained the same color as when he'd first arrived and Nate briefly wondered if it was nighttime, but there was some kind of illumination because he could see everything as clearly as if it were daytime.

Buildings stood tall against the tawny backdrop of the sky as Nate walked down the street, deeper into the city. The buildings weren't skyscraper tall, but he wouldn't want to take a drive off of any of them. No people walked the streets. It was as if he was in a ghost town, and he half expected a tumbleweed to blow down the street.

Nate tried to look into the dark windows of the buildings as he threaded through the streets, but he was unable to make out even the faintest outline of anything on the other side.

The sound of large beating wings floated down to Nate's ears, causing him to look up. Three gargoyles landed heavily on the ground behind him and he turned around to face them.

"Hands in the air!" His voice was scratchy and he stood

slightly in front of the other two. He had the face of a lion, but with a shorter snout, and charcoal gray skin.

Nate released a nervous chuckle. "Fuck that."

"Do you resist?" His ears pulled back against his head like a dog preparing to attack.

"I'm not raising my hands," Nate said. "Take it how you take it."

The lead gargoyle actually hiked up a pair of dark blue pants. Wings flaring out behind him, the gargoyle charged Nate like a bullet flying from the barrel of a gun.

Raising a fist in an uppercut, Nate connected with the gargoyle's snout before its momentum bowled him over. Both Nate and the gargoyle tumbled to the ground in a heap. The other two started to move in, but Nate was already hopping up to his feet.

Staring at his two opponents, Nate took in their features. The gargoyle on his left had the face of a crocodile but with a shortened, subdued snout. And on his right he saw the face of a rhesus monkey. They both wore the same dark blue pants as the first.

Crocface moved to grab Nate, and he delivered a knee to Crocface's abdomen before swinging a backhand to the side of Monkeyman's jaw.

Monkeyman issued a rough grunt and stumbled to the side.

Lionhead made it back to his feet and dove into Nate's back.

Feeling the impact from behind, Nate couldn't help but fall. Rolling with the momentum, he ended up on top of Lionhead and spun around until they were chest to chest.

Lionhead roared and Nate backed away from the rotten puff of air. His nostrils burned from the stench. He couldn't breathe. Lionhead's hot breath caused Nate's eyes to water.

Suddenly pulled from atop Lionhead's chest, Nate experienced a moment of weightlessness before his hands were pinned behind his back and secured. He struggled against the restraints, but his hands weren't moving.

Nate's heart dropped to his stomach as the gargoyle clamped a pair of strong, three fingered hands across his chest and took to the air. He wasn't afraid of heights, but the roller-coaster-like effect of the takeoff made Nate a little nervous. It was like being thrown out of a slingshot with the force of a bullet.

The flight was brief and the landing soft as they touched down in front of a nondescript brick building with a solid steel door. *Station 42* was written in green paint on a dark, iron plate above the entryway.

Nate was thrust toward the door and it opened just as he thought he was going to crash into it, face first. Stumbling through the door, Nate found his footing on a dark gray, concrete floor that had been worn smooth. He walked a few steps to a desk at the insistence of the gargoyle at his back that he'd come to realize was Monkeyman after they'd landed.

The desk was empty, and Nate stood there in front of it as Lionhead went around and took a seat on the other side.

"What's your name?" Lionhead's scratchy voice was like steel wool to Nate's ears.

"Nate."

"What are you doing here?"

"That's my business." Nate had a natural distrust of creatures he had never seen before.

"Answer me!" Lionhead bellowed as his fists pounded the table.

"You ever heard the phrase 'do unto others?' You attack me on the street, kidnap me, and then expect me to answer your questions like a good little boy?" Nate's anger began to rise. "No. What's going to happen here is I'm going to kill all of you. Then I'm going to walk out of here and go on about my business."

Raising a finger and pointing it toward a door in a yellowed wall behind the desk, Lionhead said, "Take him to the cage and leave him until he feels like talking."

Monkeyman directed Nate to the door and they walked through it into a room with bare, exposed stone walls to either side and a row of floor to ceiling bars at the back.

Crocface produced a key and stuck it into an ancient lock, opening the cell, and Nate was haphazardly tossed inside.

He didn't realize that his hands had been freed until they touched the floor and broke his fall, preventing him from face-planting on the dark concrete.

Nate heard the cell door close and the sounds of soft, retreating footsteps before he had a chance to raise his head.

Regaining his feet, he looked around the cell. There were no bunks, no benches. No toilet. Only a small hole carved into the floor to expel waste. There was only one other thing in the cell. Nate assumed 'thing' was the right word.

A leprechaun.

Nate almost burst out laughing. It was so unmistakably a leprechaun right down to the red hair and green suit. The only difference between this leprechaun and the cartoon versions he remembered from his childhood was the height. This leprechaun looked him eye to eye. And, maybe, the shoes. For some reason, Nate had an image of pointy, black shoes with a silvery buckle, but this leprechaun wore black Converse All Stars.

"You're a leprechaun." A hint of wonder was in Nate's voice.

"And you're a nephilim." His voice was nasally. "What of it?"

Touché!

"What is this?" Nate asked. "They have a jail in the underworld?"

The leprechaun shrugged. "They don't where you're from?"

Nate's face held a quizzical look. "How do you know..."

Once again, his shoulders shrugged. "We don't see many of your kind around these parts. I'm Josiah, by the way."

Fuck.

How could everyone tell that Nate was a nephilim? It was as if he were walking around with a sign hanging from his neck, as if he had a neon arrow pointing at his forehead.

A loud boom resonated from the front of the building, shaking the entire structure. Followed by another and another.

"What's going on?" Nate asked.

Josiah shifted from foot to foot and his eyes widened with fear. He was visibly nervous. "They're coming for me."

"Who?" Nate asked. "Who's coming?"

He wasn't sure if leprechauns were a nervous lot, but the way Josiah was acting had Nate on edge.

Another boom sounded, this one louder than the first three. Crocface's head momentarily peeked through the door, then disappeared as the door closed.

Boom!

This one shook the building as none before. It sounded like whoever was outside was trying to crash through the heavy, metal front door.

Josiah was pacing, eyes darting around like he was looking for something. Maybe an exit, an escape.

The front door gave, and the sounds of a fierce battle filtered back to them from up front. Grunts, groans, and the occasional scream could be heard.

And they were trapped in this cage. If they could breach the front door then surely these bars would pose no problem.

32

JASON

We had traveled for three days without encountering a single person. On the morning of the fourth we woke up to a dense fog covering the land.

I had slept beneath a pecan tree, and as I crawled from my sleeping bag my eyes went to Miranda's tent. Convinced that she was still asleep, I glanced toward Crush and Jael, passed out beneath a tree not far from her tent.

After ducking off to relieve myself, I strolled down to the river near our camp to get water for coffee. It was early and the sun had yet to burn off the fog, but the sky was a bright, clear blue with white puffs of cloud dotted across the cerulean backdrop.

Dipping a can into the gray water, I watched as the river diverted a small part of itself into my can, and I thought about how with every interaction we have we give up a piece of ourselves.

I saw a movement beneath the water and I thought it was a fish coming to the surface for a tasty snack, but long hair broke the surface and I watched as it continued to rise. The hair slowly turned, revealing first the profile, then a direct view of the face the hair belonged to.

Miranda looked at me with eyes that revealed nothing as she moved in my direction, climbing from the refreshing depths of the river.

As naked as the day she was born.

"You act like you've never seen a woman before." She walked over to a pile of clothes I hadn't noticed on the ground, her movements lithe and confident. "Close your mouth. You're going to catch a fly."

Hadn't even realized I was staring and I self-consciously closed my jaws with an audible *clack*.

"Oh. Don't tell me... You haven't..." She giggled. "That would have been the first thing I would have done."

The can was full, but I didn't rise.

Miranda dressed, her eyes boring into me the entire time. And she was in no hurry. "We should get back to camp."

"Go ahead," I managed. "I'll be there in a minute."

"But your can is full." She pointed.

I maintained my position squatting next to the river. "I said I'll be there in a minute."

"You're cute." Miranda smiled and turned toward camp. "Suit yourself."

She disappeared and I stood. I was frustrated. Irked because my body responded to Miranda the way it did and I had no control over it. My dick was as hard as a week old biscuit, and I didn't want her to know she had that kind of effect on me.

Slowly making my way back to camp, I gave myself a moment to recover.

Crush was up and had a fire going so I threw the can on top so it could heat up. Jael emerged from a copse of bushes from what I assumed was his morning relief and sat cross-legged in front of the fire. Miranda stepped from her tent carrying strips of beef jerky and handed one to each of us.

I abstained from the coffee, instead letting my water cool down as I chewed on the tough strips of meat.

After our silent breakfast we started packing up our things so we could get on the road while the horses grazed and drank.

"I thought I saw chimney smoke in the distance while I was washing up this morning." Miranda interrupted the silence.

"Then we'll actually see some other people today," Crush said. "I'm tired of your ugly mugs being the only ones I see."

"Sounds like somebody's getting lonely," Jael shot back.

"My man, I will never be lonely as long as I have memories of your mother to comfort me through the long nights."

Jael chuckled. "Good luck with that. My mother looks like a gremlin."

"Boys, boys." Miranda's voice was stern. "We will *not* disrespect anyone's mother. Not even your own."

Jael threw his hands up in surrender. "He started it."

Snap!

The sound of a twig cracking reached my ears and my eyes shot toward the noise. There shouldn't have been anything in that area heavy enough to snap a twig. Another stick broke, then I heard the sound of leaves brushing against each other as something heavy moved through.

Grabbing the Scythe and holding it at my side, I said, "Heads up guys! Something's coming."

Everyone jumped to their feet. Crush drew a broadsword and held it at the ready. Jael had a mean looking curved blade in his hand.

We waited.

The drumming of my heart beat filled my ears. Whatever it was, it was taking its time. I had the urge to run into the brush and confront it.

But I held my position.

33

BRIT

Small, golf cart like vehicles zipped up and down the street as they walked around to get familiar with the layout of Elan. It wasn't what one would call busy, but it was more activity than Brit was used to. Even Gutenberg didn't have this much activity. Then again, they'd also been dealing with the virus the entire time she was there.

Elan was alive. It seemed as if someone was hawking some variety of goods on almost every street corner. Foot traffic was heavy and made Brit think that everyone had somewhere to go.

This wasn't a tall city, more a sleepy college town, but over-crowded instead of sleeping. There were a number of apartment buildings and even most of the houses, which were largely made of brick, had rooms to be rented.

Sanjay, the royal guard Robert, and Brit walked past a college campus that looked to still have some activity. It was mid-afternoon. They'd arrived at the city a few hours ago, around midday. She had almost expected to feel some ominous energy looming over the city of Elan, but that wasn't the case.

Elan was pleasant. Brit had dreamed of living in a place like this. This was what society looked like. From the remote inn she'd been at it was hard to believe something like this even existed. But it did and she was there.

The college was a large enough place to hold a village full of people. The only place she'd seen so far. They still had a good amount of ground to cover. But this deserved further attention.

"That'd be a good place to keep them." Sanjay tilted his chin toward the campus.

He'd read her mind.

"I agree." Robert's voice was thoughtful. "We'll come back and have a look after the sun goes down. We should try to cover as much ground as possible while there's still light. We may find other possibilities too."

Britt hadn't quite known what to expect when Robert first told her of their mission to Elan. Being a royal guard, she had expected him to be a royal pain in the ass. But he turned out to be quite pleasant. Not to mention he was easy on the eyes. Almost as handsome as Jason.

She actually missed Jason, and as they walked the streets of Elan, she wondered what adventures he was having in this post-apocalyptic version of the wild west. The fact that she missed him was surprising. She can't remember ever missing anyone outside of her immediate family, and it was an odd feeling. Something she would have to get used to.

But now she needed to focus on the mission at hand. Tristan was in danger. Her friend. And Nana. People needed her; they were relying on her. Brit had never really had a lot of friends, but now that she did, she was determined not to let them down.

34

JASON

A figure emerged from the cover of leaves and branches. It was a man. His skin held a bluish-gray cast. His eyes were dead, yet simultaneously alive with hunger. He was followed by another, and another. Soon, a whole group of them were emerging.

The virus had spread beyond Gutenberg. The proof was right in front of me.

Holstering the Scythe, I wrapped my hand around the grip of the machete. Wielding it in front of me, I stepped toward the first zombie and swung the machete in a forty-five degree arc, connecting right above its ear. The zombie fell to the ground, soon followed by the top of its head.

My attack acted as the bang at the beginning of a race, sparking Crush and Jael into motion. As the group moved forward we held the line, slashing and stabbing as they continued to come.

Two slipped past and I glanced back to see Miranda with a dagger in her hand. It was fancy, about a foot long with a large ruby in the pommel. She looked confused about which one to attack. Lunging at the zombie on her right, Miranda stabbed it in the throat. The zombie kept coming, and realizing her mistake she withdrew the dagger and pushed it into the zombie's eye.

By that time the other zombie was on her, a woman with an indistinguishable color of hair that was falling from her head in clumps. Miranda held a forearm to the zombie's throat as it bit at the air in front of her face.

Pulling my machete from the top of a zombie's head, I raced over to her and yanked the zombie from on top of Miranda by the neck of its shirt. The zombie landed on its back and I swung the blade of my machete across the bridge of its nose.

Miranda scurried backwards before standing, and I rejoined the fight. There were about twenty altogether and before long they all lay in a pile of bodies upon a green carpet of vegetation.

My eyes roamed over my three roadies. "Everyone ok?"

They all nodded.

"We need to be going." Miranda gestured toward Jael, her breathing ragged. "Gather our horses. Let's get out of here."

I didn't say anything, but I had recognized a few of those faces as being from the Coven of Lilith. I couldn't say for certain that all of those zombies came from the Coven, but this made me think it possible they could have suffered an outbreak.

We left the gore behind, riding in the direction of the smoke Miranda had seen.

Although the sun was high in the sky when the first faint outlines of a homestead came into view, it was still well before noon. The terrain was bare, just grass, and I was sure that whoever lived there had their eyes on us well before we were capable of being an actual threat.

Large, gray mountains extended into the clouds, providing a breathtaking background for the homestead. The land was bare of trees and I wondered if that was the natural landscape, or if it was by design.

A waist high, barbed wire fence protected the property from intruders and we stopped outside the barrier and waited for someone to show themselves.

Crush spun his horse around. "Maybe no one's home."

There weren't any active signs of life, but a few things did stand out to me as clues of recent habitation. The grass within the fence line wasn't wild like the grass beyond. The doors, windows, and roof were all intact and led me to believe that someone was doing regular maintenance on the worn, wood slat house.

"Anyone home?" I called. "We don't mean any harm. Just been traveling for a few days and could really use any help we can get."

No response. Nothing moved.

Miranda's eyes met mine. "Crush may be right."

My head shook. "No. Someone's here."

I couldn't put into words how I knew, I just did. Aside from the indicators I saw, I could feel a presence. There wasn't a doubt in my mind that we were being watched.

Miranda's eyes held mine a moment longer before she climbed from her saddle and stepped up to the barbed wire, both hands spread wide in order to highlight her nonthreatening-ness. "Good morning. I'm Princess Miranda of Gutenberg. We come in peace."

The front door burst open, causing me to jump at the sudden movement. A girl of about eight or nine came flying out, pulling up short of leaving the porch.

"Princess?" the girl asked.

Miranda gave the girl a big smile. "Yes. I-"

The door flew open again and a woman who couldn't have been a day over twenty-five stepped onto the porch. "Your pop is gonna kill you! You're not supposed to talk to strangers! Get back in the house."

"We don't mean anyone any harm. Only want to ask a

couple questions. That's it, and we'll be on our way." Miranda stepped even closer to the fence.

"We don't talk to strangers." Thin fingers combed through unkept hair. "Now get on!"

"Have you had any other visitors recently? We're looking for two men." Miranda held two fingers in the air.

Turning around, the woman walked to the door, ignoring Miranda.

"Please," Miranda pleaded. "They have a weapon that can start another zombie apocalypse and possibly wipe out what's left of humanity. We have to find them. Help us."

The porch issued a squeak as she stopped. Her head spun toward us. "There are two ways to cross the mountain. One is much faster and just as dangerous. The other will take you some time, but you'll get to the other side safe. I don't know which way they went."

After giving us directions to both routes through the mountain, she stepped into the house and slammed the door so hard I could have sworn that I felt the vibration.

Miranda climbed back onto her horse and looked at me with a sly smile. "I'm thinking fast and hard. Slow and easy will put us behind when we need to be ahead."

We made camp for the night at the foot of the mountain and woke up early the next morning to start our trek up the mountain. The pale rock was loose beneath our feet and we had to lead the horses single file so they didn't injure themselves.

The incline steepened, but thankfully the footing became a little more stable and I worried less about sliding back down the mountain.

It barely felt as if we had made any progress although the sun had reached its highest point in the sky. The air was cooler and a wind blew, causing me to put my head down against its chill.

Noticing the gradient begin to level out, I was thinking that this would be a good time to take a break.

But the path had dead-ended.

We all looked at each other, confused. Had the woman intentionally misled us? But it didn't make sense that she would do that when we could just retrace our steps back down the mountain, across the plain, and right to her door.

"Bitch set us up." Jael was fuming.

Walking to the rock face, I ran my hand across its uneven surface. Squatting and standing, then stepping to the side to repeat the process, I found nothing.

I took a few steps back and stared at the wall of ancient stone.

Crush was standing there looking at me with a grin that said everything about how much he was enjoying my boyish quest to find some fantastical magic door.

My failed quest.

"We just wasted a whole fucking day." The scar across Jael's lips turned a blanched white as he pressed them together.

A shower of stones pelted us and we ducked behind our horses for cover, but they reared and kicked under the onslaught. When the mountain monsoon passed we looked up to see that we were surrounded. The high sun glinted off of steel no matter which direction I turned. The path back down the mountain had been cut off.

Miranda, Crush, and Jael all drew steel of their own.

Looking at my horse, my eyes scanned to where I'd had to put together a makeshift rig since the average saddle didn't provide the necessary accommodations. Loosening the rig, I wrapped my hand around the familiar, metal shaft.

Then I fired up the e-spear.

35

NATE

"Please," Josiah grabbed the front of Nate's shirt in both of his hands. "You gotta help me."

"Man, I don't even know what's going on." Removing Josiah's hands from the front of his shirt, Nate took a step back. "You want my help, you need to start talking. Who was that trying to bust through the door. Who is that in there engaged in fierce battle with the gargoyles? Why are you so afraid?"

With his entire body shaking, Josiah leaned his forehead against the bars. "There's nowhere to run."

Nate kindly removed a hand from Josiah's face with his own left hand, then slapped Josiah across the cheek with his right. The sharp smack resounded against the background noise of the battle. "Get your shit together and tell me what the fuck is going on. That's the only way we're going to make it out of this. That's the only way I'm going to be able to help you. So quit your cowardly ass crying and tell me who we're dealing with. Plus, ain't you supposed to be magical or something?"

Josiah's eyes flashed with anger, then settled into resignation. "Knights of Darkness."

"Like, with shining armor?"

"No. Well, kind of." Josiah glanced at the door. "They were commissioned by Lucifer himself, before..."

"Before what?"

"No one's seen him in almost five hundred years. Now the Knights of Darkness terrorize the underworld while they look for a way topside."

If these were really Lucifer's personal knights then they must be extremely powerful. And Nate thought it would be best to avoid them.

The bars were set about six inches apart. Grabbing two bars in his hands, Nate pulled with all his might, trying to spread them apart far enough to slip through.

He got nothing. They didn't budge, not even a millimeter.

Nate stepped back, looking at the bars. "Are these steel?"

"Aye," Josiah replied.

Nate had brought down a building before and he was certain it had steel in it. He had been aware of his otherworldly strength for years and this should have been a piece of cake. Why were his powers failing him now?

He was in another world.

Maybe his powers had been nullified once he had crossed over into the underworld. Something like gravity when you went into outer space. Your weight became weightless.

Why not? If there were gargoyles flying around, he guessed anything was possible here.

But if he wasn't strong enough to bend the bars...

Now Nate looked around the cell in a bit of a panic. Nothing but stone and steel. He could find no obvious weaknesses. And why should he? It was a cell. Designed for the specific intent and purpose of holding people - and leprechauns - so they couldn't escape.

The door flew inward and landed with a dull thump in the middle of the room. The Knights of Darkness revealed themselves.

Two of them stepped through the door, and Nate studied them intently. They were hard to describe because it was almost as if they were nothing. Nate got the impression of a long black robe or cloak on each of them, but it was as if they were made of smoke. Or a shimmering mirage. Their visage went in and out of existence, not as a whole, but as wisps of smoke would.

An energy emanated from them, reminding Nate of a lightsaber in a Star Wars movie he remembered watching as a kid. Almost as if they were energy themselves.

Nate was afraid, and he was totally unaccustomed to that feeling. Adrenaline flooded his system and his heart rate kicked up. Beads of sweat appeared on his brow and his hands were slick.

The fear did it. Nate's eyes glowed bright blue-white, as if his pupils were a pair of halogen headlights. Raising his head toward the stone ceiling, Nate lifted his hands.

The foundation shook beneath their feet and the vibrations carried through the walls and ceiling.

A resonant, baritone voice surrounded Nate. "The leprechaun. We want the leprechaun."

Josiah moved behind Nate, shielding himself from the Knights, but as the shaking of the building increased in intensity he thought better of it and moved back to his previous spot. Really, Josiah didn't know what to do, so he just repeated a mantra over and over. "Oh, my god. Oh, my god. Oh, my god."

"Foolish man. Cease your parlor tricks and give us the leprechaun."

Nate didn't know which of the Knights spoke for he saw no mouths from which they could speak.

Although Nate heard their words he wouldn't be stupid enough to believe them. How could he trust them? He couldn't trust anyone in this world because he didn't yet understand the dynamics of this world.

Rock dust filled the air as the acute earthquake shifted the tectonic plates of each stone that comprised *Station 42*. Stones the size of pebbles broke off and fell. Pebbles soon became rocks. Rocks soon became chunks.

Josiah's mantra increased in volume. "Oh, my god. Oh, my god. Oh, my god."

The back wall began to crumble in earnest. A breeze could be felt at Nate's back as air was drawn in through the disintegrating barrier.

"He's going to escape." The baritone voice again, right before one of the Knights moved toward the bars and attacked the steel with a great war-hammer and a speed that made him almost invisible.

The clank of steel against steel resonated and echoed, mixing with the sounds of rocks colliding with the concrete floor. Sparks flew where the hammer made contact with the bars, and they began to bend.

A hole opened up in the wall large enough for a man to fit, and Josiah ran toward it, dodging the falling debris. Diving through the cavity, he looked back and yelled at Nate, "Come on!"

But Nate wasn't finished.

Another strike of hammer upon steel. More sparks flew. The bars were weakening.

"What are you doing?" Josiah screamed. "Let's get out of here!"

The back wall was now a pile of rubble and completely compromised, unable to support the weight of the roof. It started to give, the unsupported weight bowing in the middle, creating a V with a long crack running down the center from the back of the building.

Then the roof caved in. Suddenly. In its entirety. There was no progression from one end to another. The whole thing just came down in one big heap.

Nate looked around, and just as the last time, he was untouched. It appeared as if Nate had been standing inside a cylindrical tube as the ceiling collapsed and he felt like he'd fallen down a well.

After climbing atop the rubble, he looked down and saw josiah.

"You're alive!" Josiah exclaimed. "But we gotta go! You may have slowed them down a bit, but they don't die."

"What the fuck is going on?" Nate jumped from the debris. "Why are they after you? What did you do?"

36

BRIT

The moon was waxing in its first quarter, but provided enough light for Robert, Sanjay, and Brit to see as they infiltrated the campus without being too conspicuous. Crossing the open expanse of lawn that led to the massive main building, they stuck to the shadows, avoiding the periodically spaced overhead lights that gave the main walkways a sense of security.

Staying away from the main entrance, the trio skirted the front of the building to the large auditorium on its left side. They paused at the corner at the end of the building. After looking down the side of the auditorium and confirming that the coast was clear they crept down the side toward the rear of the building.

At the back, a walkway forked off in three directions, each leading to what Brit assumed had been dormitories. To her right, and further away, were apartment style buildings that had most likely been intended for upperclassmen.

They moved toward the first triplet of quad level brick buildings. No lights could be seen behind any of the windows. Either everyone was asleep, or nobody was home.

A light was above the door and there was no way to avoid it, so they just had to be quick about getting in. Robert stepped to the door and turned the knob, only to find that it was locked. Pulling a slim, yet sturdy card from his pocket, he slid it between the door and jamb until the lock gave.

They slipped inside and Sanjay quietly shut the door behind them.

The hallway was dark so Sanjay pulled a small flashlight from his pocket and turned it on.

They were standing directly in front of stairs leading to the second level and a step to the right put them in front of a hallway that led to the back.

Brit saw the remnants of an old spider web in the corner above the door before they moved off down the hall. Laying her ear against the first door they came to, she listened. Not a sound to be heard.

Turning the knob, she opened the door a fraction of an inch and tried to peek into the darkness. But she couldn't distinguish anything so she slowly opened the door wide enough for her head to fit through. Then wide enough for her body.

Robert and Sanjay followed and they looked around, using the light filtering in through a small window.

The room was full of books. Stacks and stacks of them. It looked like someone had robbed a library and used this place as their secret stash.

They looked at each other, amazed, shaking their heads. No villagers in this room.

After moving back into the hall and pulling the door up, they heard the unmistakable jingle of keys being put into a lock.

Somebody was coming into the building.

They immediately shuffled back into the room just as the door was opening. Had they been seen? Did they make it in time? Did they make a sound as they closed the door?

A thin streak of light filtered through the threshold as whoever entered the building turned on a light. The sounds of footballs could be heard as they passed the door, whistling an unfamiliar tune.

After the steps faded, they waited a few minutes in the deafening silence, each second ticking away at the pace of a sloth. Certain the coast was clear, Brit followed Robert and Sanjay into the hall and out the door into the illumination of the porch light.

As soon as they were safely out the door they took off running in the direction of the apartments. Maybe they could get lost in an area where people were expected to be.

Breathing hard, they arrived on the blacktop between two rows of buildings, each one consisting of four apartments, two on the ground level and two up top.

As Brit eyed the buildings she realized that they were oddly unoccupied. That didn't make much sense considering what seemed to be a city with more people than space. But it was obvious that these had been empty for some time.

"They're not here." Sanjay's voice held a hint of disappointment.

The only other place Brit had seen large enough to house a village was a temple, but there was no way people were staying in the temple with all of the activity that she'd remembered seeing.

37

NATE

Josiah's head shook side to side. "Assholes are after my pot of gold."

The Knights of Darkness wanted this leprechaun named Josiah for his pot of gold. This had to be a dream, or some kind of drug induced delirium. Nate remembered the Noid blowing a powder in his face. Maybe he was still experiencing the effects. "You can't be serious. You really have a fucking pot of gold?"

"Of course I have one!" He was incredulous. "Every leprechaun does."

"So why do they want gold? They gonna buy a yacht and sail around the world? Go to the strip club and make it rain? What am I missing?"

"The legend is true." The sound of his hands clapping together was surprisingly loud in the silence. "You've heard it right? There's a pot of gold at the end of every rainbow. Another little known fact about them is that they are bridges, leading from one place to another. My gold happens to be in the underworld."

"And the rainbow is in my world." Nate thought he was beginning to understand. "They're trying to get topside."

They walked down the quiet, dark street. The place was abandoned, hopeless. Stoic residences stared at them with blank windows and untamed lawns. Nate wondered about that. There was no sun. No moon or stars either. How was grass growing without the sun?

"And they'll do anything to get there." Josiah stopped and eyed Nate. "So what are you doing here? What's your story?"

Nate wondered if he could trust this leprechaun, but in reality he needed help. He didn't have a clue where he was going and it didn't look like there were crowds of people lining up to offer assistance.

"I'm going to Hambrathia." Nate had an idea. "Help me get there and you'll have my protection from the Knights. Then, let me cross your bridge to go home. We can work together."

"Hambrathia is desolate." The leprechaun shivered. "Why would you want to go there?"

"I need the Poppy of Paradise."

Nate could see the wheels turning in Josiah's head. Would he accept Nate's offer? It was obvious he was scared out of his mind and it didn't seem like the Knights would stop their pursuit.

"Aye." Josiah smiled. "You have a deal."

Lonely homes became forlorn trees as they left the residential area behind. Nothing like being surrounded by trees in the dark to raise the hairs on the back of your neck. At least they were walking in the middle of the street.

"You know, Michael Jordan shot 83% from the line."

"Huh?" Nate was caught off guard by the random comment.

"Michael Jordan. You've never heard of Michael Jordan?" Josiah's head tilted questioningly. "He hit 83% of all his free throws. That's incredible. You ever shot a free throw? Looks easy, but it ain't."

"Basketball?"

"I love that round ball." Josiah mimed taking a shot. "You play? You kinda look like Kyrie."

"I haven't had much time for sports. Spent most of my life just trying to survive." Kicking at a loose pebble, Nate raised his head toward the eerie sky.

And that was when he felt it. Something was watching. Something dangerous and hungry. Nate didn't have to see it to know it was there. He felt it, felt it's hunger. His heart thudded as all kinds of physiological alarm bells went off.

"You okay?" Josiah asked after realizing Nate was no longer beside him.

He had forgotten all about Josiah, so intense was the feeling emanating from this covert stalker. His focus had been complete, in a way that only evolution could ingrain in the psyche from some primitive experience with a savage, primitive threat.

"We should keep moving." Walking to Nate, Josiah followed his eyes toward the tree line. "What is it?"

Nate didn't actually see anything so he was unable to answer the question. "Let's go. Just stay on point."

Nate couldn't shake the feeling of being stalked. Whatever was in the trees was still there, quietly following, waiting for the perfect moment to strike. The anticipation was almost enough to make Nate run into the trees and confront his slyboot pursuer head on.

Fighting the urge, he kept putting one foot in front of the other.

Maybe he should listen to Josiah as he droned on about meaningless basketball stats, but no. Nate didn't want to be distracted. Slipups count and there was something in the trees waiting for him to do just that.

Stop tripping, Nate. There's probably nothing even there. Man, I'm losing my mind.

But even as Nate tried to talk himself into believing that nothing was out there, he knew better. Something was there. Of that he was certain.

Stepping into the middle of a crossroads, Nate was reminded of an old legend about making deals with the devil at a crossroads. Of men and women selling their souls to obtain their heart's desire. Temporary fulfillment in exchange for eternal... This.

He'd always thought the crossroads legend was about the decisions you make in a moment. That every decision you're faced with is a sort of crossroad, and if you choose wrong you'll face the consequences of that choice. Metaphorical as opposed to literal.

Now he wasn't so sure. Recent experience had opened his eyes to a whole 'nother world, one in which the possibility of the devil himself making deals with people wasn't so far-fetched.

A rustle of leaves. Behind and to his right.

The predator had chosen its moment.

Turning to face the threat, Nate saw a flutter of leaves. Then it emerged from the brush.

A tap on the shoulder startled Nate into turning his head. The leprechaun, Josiah, was the owner of the offending finger. But it was what Nate saw behind Josiah that made his body shake from the flood of adrenaline.

Creatures were appearing from the woods at each of the corners of the crossroads. Four in total. Fairly tall and standing on two legs covered with ragged pants, their lips were pulled back, revealing rows of sharp fangs.

"Vampires?" Nate spun around, trying to keep them all in sight.

"Vampires." Josiah confirmed.

Humanoid, with wrinkled skin and small, pointy ears, they were just plain ugly. Nate wondered about the stories showcasing their seductive violence and he couldn't see it. How would one of these hideous creatures be capable of seducing anyone?

Then Nate remembered how to kill these things. A stake to the heart. Or decapitation.

Only, Nate was fresh out of stakes and swords. "What do we do here, Josiah?"

"I don't know," Josiah shrugged. "They've never been a threat to me. Guess they don't like leprechaun blood."

Nate didn't feel as if he'd been followed. He felt as if he'd been herded, and Josiah was beginning to look like the lead sheepdog. "You led me here."

Josiah held a quizzical look. "You think that I..."

As the vampires closed in, Nate noticed that one of them had a knife jammed beneath its belt.

"You led me down this road. You knew what was in the trees when I stopped back there." Walking towards Josiah, Nate angled himself so the vampire with the knife would reach him first. "But you acted like it was nothing. You knew what was going on this whole time! I can't believe I fell for this shit."

"I swear I didn't." Josiah took a step backward. "I swear. You got to believe me. I had nothing to do with this."

"You fucking bitch ass motherfucker." Maintaining his position, Nate slammed a fist into his palm.

"I promise. You just saved me..." Josiah's eyes widened with pain. "My pot of gold..."

The vampire was almost within an arm's reach.

"You set me up!" Nate slammed a forearm into the vampire's throat and grabbed the knife with his other hand, stabbing it into the vampire's heart, but it hissed and bit and continued to attack.

Fuck, not a stake. Guess I gotta cut his head off.

The vampire tried to wrap Nate in a bearhug as he tried to figure out how to decapitate this vampire with a knife. It was imperative he figure it out as fast as possible since the other three were closing in.

Switching the knife to his defending hand, Nate grabbed the back of the vampire's head with his freshly free hand. He then slid his forearm across until the blade made contact with the vampire's neck. Pushing with his knife hand and pulling with the hand on the back of the vampire's head, Nate decapitated the monster.

The other three were soon taken care of in variations of the same maneuver. If it works, it works. No need to reinvent the wheel.

Breathing heavily, Nate turned to Josiah. "You good?"

38

JASON

"I'll be damned if I die by the hand of a half-man." Jael's scar stretched in a grimace as he stood at the ready.

We were surrounded on all sides by rock and men wielding weapons. There was no escape. Sure, we could fight our way out. I was confident in that. But we meant these people no harm.

Unless they had the virus and were intent on bathing the remains of society with the microscopic organisms.

"We don't mean you any harm." I held the e-spear down at my side. "We're just trying to pass. If we offended you in some way, I assure you that's not our intent. There doesn't have to be any blood."

One of them stepped forward. Standing about waist high, like all the others, he held a double edged axe with razor sharp blades that reflected the sun's rays.

"We should kill all these fucking dwarves." Jael was basically snarling like a rabid dog.

"We're little people, not dwarves. Neither are we midgets." The voice was stern and came from the one who had stepped forward. "State your business or I shall give your friend the opportunity he so desires."

Good. They were talking.

"Someone stole a weapon that has the potential to wipe out the rest of humanity. We're not going to let that happen. As long as you let us pass." I tried to relax and look as non-threatening as possible while everyone else stood ready for a fight.

"Tell me of this weapon," he demanded.

"Do you have the power to make the decision to let us pass?" I wasn't comfortable divulging the contents of the weapon to just anyone.

He paused. "I won't ask again. Tell me of this weapon."

He wasn't the guy in charge.

"I'll talk to your leader."

The guy whispered to another who turned and disappeared behind a rock.

After a few tense, silent minutes the man returned and whispered something to the guy with whom I'd been speaking.

"Follow me," the man said, turning and strolling off without waiting for a response.

I followed. Then Crush, Jael, and Miranda followed. Then our welcome party fell in behind them.

We traveled behind the rock and down a short path with a severe curve. The path ended at a thick and sturdy wooden door.

The dancing light of torches illuminated the inside of the cave's narrow entrance. Our boots echoed as we traversed the uneven floor down a corridor. Entering a large room, I took in the long table that dominated the space. A variety of intricate, artisan axes decorated the torch-lit walls. At the back of the room were a series of archways, but it was dark beyond so I couldn't see anything.

A man sat at the head of the table. Old and grizzled, he had a long, white beard and a severely balding head. The man was wide of stature. Solid. And short like the others.

"What are you doing on my rock?" His voice was aged and wisened. Palms flat on the table, he stared at me.

Unconsciously, I bowed my head out of respect. "A couple guys stole a weapon and we believe they headed west. A virus. Capable of wiping out what's left of civilization. We discovered this path through the mountain and took it. We're just looking to pass to the other side."

"It was after the pandemic we fled here." His eyes stared off into space for a moment. "Little people like us weren't seen as helpful to the war effort. Like we can't fight. Yet here we stand. Or sit, in my case. I'm old. Don't do much standing these days. So tell me about this virus."

A hand touched the back of my shoulder.

It was Miranda.

"It's a modified Z virus. Designed to bypass previous vaccination or immunity. Weaponized. These guys probably want to sell it and get rich."

"Huh. I agree, something like that shouldn't be floating about." He gestured at the table. "What's your name, young man? Sit. Your friends, as well."

"I'm Jason."

"Nice to meet you, Jason. I'm Orson." His toothless smile softened his eyes. "Of course you may pass. But, eat and rest here for the night and start your journey fresh in the morning."

"We really should be getting on," I explained. "We're already behind these guys and that gap is getting wider by the minute."

Miranda spoke for the first time. "Your hospitality is greatly appreciated. We'll gladly accept."

"And who are you, young lady?" Orson asked.

"Princess Miranda of Gutenberg."

"A princess, say you?" Orson's eyebrows raised in surprise.

Miranda nodded. "And these are my guards, Crush and Jael."

The table was big enough for almost everyone and all the seats were quickly filled. We engaged in small talk as a meal was being prepared.

But it wasn't long before large platters were being hauled to the table.

"You're in for a real treat tonight. The guys got lucky and got a deer. Roast venison and vegetables." Orson's face twitched, but he immediately got it under control. "Unfortunately, no bread. Our grain stores are getting frighteningly low, I'm afraid."

"Where do you get your grain?" I asked out of idle curiosity.

"When we came here we brought as much as we could store. We don't get many visitors and we're a rather reclusive lot. We've been living on the grain that came with us. Nothing lasts forever though."

"Where did y'all come from?" My eyes darted around the room. "This place seems old, like you've been here forever."

"Yes, it was quite the discovery. We come from all over. The rejects. With one thing in common." Orson looked up and down the length of the table. "We were nomads for months, adding to our numbers as we traveled. Others heard of us and came searching. Finding this cave was purely luck. Or, grave misfortune. Maybe a bit of both. One of my guys leaned against a rock and fell right in. May he rest with the gods."

The food was eaten in silence and I was hungrier than I'd realized. I couldn't tell you if it was good or not. Somewhere along the line I had heard that hunger was the best seasoning, and in this instance it applied.

After dinner, we took to rooms that had been designated to us. Room was a bit of a stretch. They were more like cells, with nothing more than a bed and a table with a bowl of water on top.

I let my mind wander aimlessly, thinking of what we might

discover next, of Miranda, of Brit. About Orson saying he barely had enough grain to feed his people. Of the fact that I was sleeping in a cave and not a cell, and how that seemed like a completely different me in a completely different life. Somewhere along the line I drifted off into a dreamless sleep.

39

NATE

It seemed like they had been walking for days, but with no sunrise or sunset Nate really didn't know. He guessed it hadn't been all bad. He'd absorbed a ton of meaningless basketball facts that he could have never imagined learning. He didn't care who'd won the championship in 1992. Nate hadn't even been born.

But now he knew.

And now they were approaching Hambrathia. At least according to Josiah. They'd been walking through a desolate, wind-blown sandscape for the past day. Nothing but the annoying, monotonous whistle of the wind and a mind numbing expanse of sand. He would have given up and gone home if he'd had the option. And as Nate shielded his eyes and stared into the horizon he didn't see that Hambrathia would be any different.

At least he wasn't thirsty. Apparently, the underworld didn't require food or water. Then he remembered that only his spirit was to make the journey.

Sure doesn't feel like I'm only here in spirit. My feet are killing me.

Nate couldn't imagine anything growing in this landscape. It was so barren it didn't seem capable of supporting any kind of life. But if Vicar said that damn poppy was here, it was here.

Another couple hours passed before Josiah alerted Nate to the fact that they were officially in Hambrathia.

Same dull landscape.

They pushed on.

The wind eased incrementally and Nate started to see dark green on the horizon. Finally. The monotony was risking his sanity. Even Josiah hadn't said anything for a while. He must have been feeling his brain turn to mush as well. For a long time it hadn't even seemed like they were making any progress. But now they had confirmation of their advancement.

Finally stepping foot into waist high head, Nate felt a sense of relief. He couldn't have been happier to be out of that god forsaken desert. And the idea of having to return through it filled him with anxiety.

The frosty white peaks of mountains could be seen in the far distance to both his right and left. They were tiny from this distance, not even really mountains. More like they were erected from a child's Lego set.

Nate was comfortable in the tall grass. The majority of Nate's independent life had been spent post-pandemic, and he'd wandered many fields that had been returned to their original, pre-societal glory. He'd actually thought it beautiful, and imagined ancient mammoths roaming the plains.

But the grass here lacked the color and vibrance he'd appreciated back in his world. All colors in this place looked muted, dark. Like someone had fiddled with the saturation and brightness of a tv. Nate often found himself squinting his eyes in an effort to force more color out of objects.

As if that would actually help.

"Smell that?" Josiah had finally found his voice again.

Now that Nate thought about it he did notice a faint stench

in the air. What was that? It almost smelled like the dead, but not quite. It had a sweet undertone, which Nate found odd. How could something so funky also smell sweet? "What is it?"

Josiah looked over at him. "The very thing you're looking for."

"So we're close?"

"Soon." Josiah trampled a bit of grass. "The wind carries the scent down the valley. It'll be much stronger once we get there. Unmistakable. You'll know."

They trudged on through the grass. This would be great territory for snakes, but Nate didn't believe that the snakes he was familiar with were the serpents of this world.

"So why do you need it?"

Josiah's question pulled Nate from his thoughts. "I don't. Not personally."

Josiah looked at him questioningly. "So you came to the underworld, risking life and limb for something you don't even need?"

"You talk a lot. Has anybody ever told you that?" Nate asked.

"Why?" Josiah pressed. "Why would you go to all that trouble for something you don't even need?"

Nate knew that he was just as capable as Vicar or Gerent Malbent. If they could be in charge, why couldn't he? The only difference between them and him was that they had an army. At least for now. Malbent told Nate that he would lead the army against Gutenberg. That's how he would get his army. Take theirs right from under their noses.

Then he would start his own kingdom. One where people like Nate, people with his skin and hair, people who had been marginalized for time immemorial, and people who only wanted to live as equals could do just that.

But first, Nate had to get this poppy. "You gotta do what you gotta do."

The stink started to overwhelm Nate's senses and his

stomach churned. This must have been what Josiah had been talking about. New notes had been added. A strong astringent scent that made Nate think about the flavor of coffee. Beneath that, a smell he often associated with fungus.

Still no poppy.

He couldn't imagine the smell getting any worse. His eyes were already watering.

Then he saw a single blue flower surrounded by seven brown, wrinkled pods. Nate was so happy he could have done a backflip. He'd found this poppy and now he could get the hell out of here.

Cutting the seven pods and the flower, Nate quickly stuffed them into a small pouch. A sense of accomplishment washed over him.

He looked over at Josiah, smiling. "Now we go to your pot of gold so I can get back home."

"Indeed. My pot of gold."

Turning to retrace their steps, Nate froze mid-turn. The visage of three forms, not solid, but... there. Existing, but not quite. Like a trick of the eye.

Knights of Darkness.

"Hand over the leprechaun and we'll forgive your earlier transgression." The voice sent vibrations through Nate's bones. "Refuse and you'll spend the rest of eternity wishing you had done otherwise."

Not this. Not now. As soon as Nate had found his prize, the reason for this jaunt into the underworld, as soon as he'd pocketed this damned poppy and could head back home, he had to deal with this shit.

Nate's heart and stomach dropped to his ankles as the blood thumped energetically through his veins. He was both afraid and angry. Afraid because he had no building to bring down on the Knight's heads and no other ideas of how to slow them down. Angry because they were here, at Nate's moment of accomplishment, attempting to derail his plans and prevent him from returning home with the object of his quest.

The anger overwhelmed the fear, and Nate also knew that aggression of violence and striking first was always a good strategy.

Charging the Knights with nothing but the knife he'd used to decapitate the vampires, Nate slashed and sliced at the first one he reached. The blade went through clean. A little too clean. There was absolutely no resistance whatsoever. It was as if he'd tried to cut through smoke.

The knight appeared behind him. Just like that. One moment he'd been in front of Nate and the next he was behind.

Nate felt a crushing blow against his back and he fell forward, but kept his footing. Rising into the air, his stomach roiled as if he were on a roller coaster. Then he was thrown to the side, this time landing on his back.

Attempting to get up, Nate realized he was pinned. He struggled against the force, but got nothing for his efforts. There was nothing he could do but lie there and watch the three Knights of Darkness as they closed in.

40

JASON

After a morning meal with Orson and a table full of people, we set off on our way.

One of Orson's guys led us down a long stairway, one that I thought would never end. We finally reached the bottom and exited the cave at the base of the mountain.

Taking in a short meadow, I saw our horses, saddled and grazing on the green grass.

"Your horses are ready," the man said. "Travel safe. I hope you find your virus."

As soon as we'd rode into the tree line, Jael said, "We couldn't have left that place soon enough."

"What did they ever do to you?" Crush sounded bored. "Lose your first girlfriend to a little person or something?"

Jael's disposition was cloudy as he rode next to Crush and ahead of me and Miranda, but he made no response.

We rode through an endless expanse of wilderness and made camp two nights in a row. On the afternoon of the third day we saw signs of civilization. Inhabited farms on rural roads were the first indications we were nearing a town or city.

Soon, we passed more homes in small community clusters

of pre-pandemic architecture. Three wide eyed children were playing near the road, and as we passed they stopped and stared until we were out of sight. They must not have been accustomed to seeing new faces travel through.

The sun was blindingly bright in my eyes as it made its afternoon descent, and that was when we were approaching the city proper. No defensive wall surrounded the city. There was no guarded gate through which to pass. Just a steady progression from rural to suburban to urban.

The only outstanding thing separating this world from the pre-pandemic world was that instead of cars everyone traveled the same way we did. By horseback. And those who weren't riding either walked or pedaled bicycles.

"I could go for a bite to eat and a drink." Crush pointed toward a white building with the words 'Turtle Island Bar & Grill' above a frosted glass door.

"I've been seeing turtles everywhere." Miranda looked at me. "Did you notice? In yards, on the street lights. Now this bar, but it says Turtle Island. I don't remember crossing any water."

I hadn't noticed the turtles and I didn't remember crossing a body of water either. "I'm too hungry to notice much of anything except the growling of my stomach. But we definitely didn't cross water. I'd remember that."

The inside of the bar was cozy even though it was largely empty. The bar's busiest hours were yet to come and I appreciated that fact. We wouldn't have to wait long to be served.

A waitress appeared at the table we'd taken for ourselves and handed out menus and took our order for drinks. As I gave my preference, her eyes lingered on mine a moment too long, causing me to really look at her. About medium height with rich brown skin, her hair was twisted in locks that hung to her shoulders. She was definitely attractive.

After the waitress left I noticed Miranda looking at me rather curiously so I asked, "What's up?"

"Nothing," was all she said in response.

The waitress returned with our drinks, flashing a bright smile as she set a glass in front of me.

"Mind if I ask you a question?" I figured I might as well ask about the virus since I had her attention. "We came a long way looking for two guys who are rumored to be selling a weaponized Z virus. I know people tend to be loose of the tongue in bars. Have you heard any whispers?"

Her expression went from intrigued at the possibility of what I might ask to stoic and closed off. Her face was so hard to read I wondered if she was a poker player. She could simply be used to shutting down as patrons made passes at the pretty bar waitress. Or I could have asked the wrong question.

"No," she simply answered, before turning around and disappearing into the kitchen.

"Somebody looks a little guilty." Crush brushed his own set of long locs back with a hand. "I bet she knows something. I was starting to think she had a crush on my man, Jason. From the look on her face you royally screwed that up!"

Crush's laughter filled the sparsely patronized bar.

Miranda had an elbow on the table with her chin in her palm, staring at me. Her face was just as closed off as the waitress's.

Our food arrived and the chill was still emanating from our waitress. I wondered if she really did know something. Oh, well. It looked like that ship had already sailed.

But if there was a possibility that she knew something, others would as well.

After our meal, we left. The sun was just dipping behind the horizon and activity in the bar was picking up. After considering questioning others in the bar I discarded the thought. The waitress's behavior confused me, and that made me uncomfortable.

The buildings were a mixed bag of elevations. Some of the

structures were tall, reaching for the sky, while others were shorter and bathed in the shadows of the larger edifices. Some were pre-pandemic modern and others were older, like they should have been historical sites.

I also noticed that none of the buildings, short nor tall, modern nor historic, showed signs of the destruction that was wrought upon the world during the Z Wars. Walking through the streets, it was almost easy to forget that the pandemic and wars had even happened. There were no patches or repairs that had been made to make places inhabitable. This city seemed as if it had been completely unaffected.

"Is it just me, or did we come out the other side of that mountain in Africa or something?" Crush pulled my attention from the architecture. "I haven't seen a white face since we crossed."

"Crush!" Miranda chided.

"I'm just saying."

Starting to pay more attention to the faces we passed walking through the streets, I had to admit that Crush may have been onto something. Every face I saw was some shade of brown. The spectrum ranged from the deep, rich brown of the earth to the lighter shades of tan, reddish-browns and bronzes in between.

The diversity of shades was astonishing.

The people had curly hair, straight hair, locs, and every texture in between, with colors ranging from jet black to reds to blonde. A woman passed with a head full of long, wild blonde curls and medium brown skin and I had to glance over at Miranda, their resemblance was so closely matched.

Now that I thought about it, I hadn't seen non-melanated skin since we came out of the mountain either. Could it even be possible? A city full of people who had commonly been referred to as minorities?

Then I thought back to Orson and the other little people who had banded together.

It was possible.

Up ahead, I saw a sign for a coffee shop. I wasn't a coffee drinker. It tasted like bitter water to me. But I thought it would be a great place to overhear a conspiratorial conversation. I could almost see it. Two guys huddled over steaming cups of coffee, discussing plans for the riches they would soon acquire.

"Let's stop in the coffee shop," I said as we neared the entrance.

"Miss Starbucks?" Crush asked. "You need a cuppa-frappa-lotta-whatever the hell they used to call it?"

A smile cracked Jael's scarred lips. "Coffee's the best idea anyone's had since we left Gutenberg."

Entering the front door to the jingle of a small bell, I was pleasantly assaulted by the aroma of freshly ground coffee beans.

If only coffee tasted like it smelled.

Approaching the counter, we passed booths and tables where people were grouped in hushed conversation.

"What can I get for you today?" Medium height, he had deep bronze skin and high cheekbones.

Everyone placed their orders then turned and stared at me, waiting.

"I'm good. Thanks." I glanced at his name tag. "Thomas. We're visitors here and I gotta say, this city is amazing."

"What brings you into town?" Thomas stood in front of a shiny, steel percolator.

"Two guys from back home stole a weaponized virus and we're trying to retrieve it."

A quizzical look appeared on his face with one eyebrow raised, but he said nothing. Just continued preparing the order.

Street lights were on when we stepped back into the evening air.

As we were walking along the street, getting familiar with the city, I noticed a waitress on the side of a restaurant drinking a glass of water as she leaned against the wall. Short, barely standing five feet tall, her skin was at the lighter end of the spectrum and she had a short natural.

I stopped abruptly and walked toward her. "Hey, I'm Jason. Can I ask you a quick question?"

After running my story down to her, I waited for her reaction.

I got nothing. She just continued drinking her water in silence.

Shrugging my shoulders, I turned and went back to my group.

A couple buildings from the restaurant, a voice behind us called out, "Hey! The four of you. Stop where you are!"

Pivoting toward the voice, I saw three guys wearing pre-pandemic style police uniforms with swords in their belts.

One of the men drew his sword. "You're coming with us. Queen Califa requests your presence."

41

NATE

"Stop! I'll give you the pot." Josiah's hands waved in the air, trying to get the Knight's attention. "Let him go and I'll give it to you. I give up. I'm tired of running. Shit, there's nowhere left for me to run. You can have the damned pot of gold for all I care."

The Knights of Darkness faced Josiah, although Nate's limbs remained restricted.

Josiah was going to give them the gold to save Nate. It was a nice gesture and Nate appreciated it, but that would be releasing a whole new level of terror upon mankind.

Nate couldn't let that happen.

He started to feel it. The energy coursing through his body. He'd learned early on to never let it completely out, to restrain the power within him. It was uncontrollable, Nate was a passenger in his own body whenever the other part of him took over. All he could do was sit back, watch, and try to enjoy the ride.

But in this situation, Nate didn't see any other option.

Nate just let go, let that other part of him have free reign.

Light shone from his eyes, a brilliant blue-white. His hands started to move. Then his arms.

Nate sat up.

The three Knights wheeled around, confused. There was no way Nate should have been able to move. But he was.

Raising his hands toward one of the Knights like Ken and Ryu throwing a fireball, Nate raised his arms to the sky and the Knight rose into the air, tendrils of itself trailing like contrails behind an airplane.

Josiah looked on in amazement, jaw hanging to the ground.

One of the other Knights moved toward Nate, and he directed an arm his way. The Knight froze, unable to move, as Nate had just been.

Yeah, the rabbit had the gun now.

Nate smashed the airborne Knight into the frozen Knight as he brought his hands together. The resounding clarp was like thunder, echoing throughout the valley. Two Knights became one in a cloud of dust, or smoke, or whatever the hell they were made of.

One remained. He drew a sword, and Nate admired its power from the passenger seat of his body. It crackled and spat as if the steel of its blade was composed entirely of electrons.

The knight charged and swung an arching slash, but Nate merely leaned to the side and let the blade slide along the contours of his body without it actually touching him.

The Knight took a step back and dropped to one knee. "I yield. At first, I doubted you were truly an archangel. But, now I am certain. I submit to your grace."

The shadow of wings spread behind Nate as he stepped toward the Knight and lay a hand atop its head. "You mistake me."

Dropping to a knee of his own, Nate pressed his palm into the soil, vanquishing the Knight in a puff of whatever.

The sword fell to the ground, its steel still crackling with the same energy as when the Knight held it.

Grabbing the hilt of the sword, Nate stood and held the vibrant blade in front of him until the shadow of wings retracted and the sword settled into being nothing more than a fancy piece of steel.

He studied it. A gold inlay ran the length of the blade. The quillon and pommel were gold with silver inscriptions, and the grip was wrapped in leather. The craftsmanship was remarkable. The grip fit perfectly in Nate's hand and the balance was perfect.

"It's an archangel's blade, possibly even Michael's," Josiah leered at the gold quillon.

"I just vanquished whatever the hell those things were." Nate took a deep breath. "I've never said 'vanquish' in my life, but I can't think of anything else to call it."

"You okay?" Josiah asked.

"That was fucking dope!" Nate laughed out loud. "Did you see that shit?"

"You kept to your end of the bargain," Josiah said. "Let's get you home."

IT WAS mid-afternoon when Nate arrived at Vicar's temple. Never had he imagined he'd be so happy to see the sun, and he reveled in its warmth. The idea of plants living without the rays of the sun was still mind blowing, but the answers to some questions were far beyond the breadth of his mind.

Pushing open the massive red doors, Nate transitioned from the imposing, gothic facade into the acoustically designed cathedral. After weaving through parishioner seating, he traversed the interior of the building, footfalls silenced by the plush, red carpet, and stood in front of the door to Vicar's office.

Nate patted the pouch to reassure himself of the poppy's presence, even though he was certain it was there.

After giving a quick knock, Nate was invited in.

Vicar was seated behind his desk and two of his aides were in chairs across from him. "Ah, Nate. You've returned. I'm assuming you have my poppy?"

42

JASON

One officer led our pack and the other two followed behind Crush, Jael, Miranda, and me as we headed toward the center of the city. After rounding a corner, we came to an iron gate that had to be at least twenty feet tall with wicked looking spikes on top. It surrounded a vast expanse of land, in the center of which sat a stepped pyramid.

To say it was huge would be a massive understatement. I felt dwarfed by its reflective glass walls. This was no ancient structure. Not at all. It was as modern as the towering steel and glass skyscrapers of New York City, if they even still existed, but not as tall.

The lead officer spoke to a guard at the gate, who then opened the gate for us to enter. The lawn was cut precisely and ornamental bushes and trees broke the monotony. As we got closer to the pyramid, I saw the walls for what they really were.

The surface was covered in solar panels.

I was amazed, and there was a moment where my quartet exchanged looks of astonishment. Certainly, I had never seen anything like it and from the looks on their faces, neither had they.

A set of stairs led to massive doors that were opened by two guards wearing the same uniforms as our escorts. Crossing an antechamber, another set of doors were opened for us and we stepped into a great hall. It was empty, devoid of seating and people, and felt cavernous. I briefly wondered how many times my voice would echo if I were to yell something.

The center of the room held a large, comfortable looking pillow on top of which sat a woman in a finely tailored, green dress. She didn't rise as we entered, merely followed our progress with bored eyes.

"It's been brought to my attention that you seek a weapon. A virus." The woman's voice was soft as her tone was hard. "Why do you seek such a thing?"

"I'm Princess Miranda of Gutenberg-"

"What do you know of being a princess?" Her eyes bored into Miranda's.

Caught off guard by the interruption, Miranda stammered. "I..."

"Thought so."

I spoke up. "Two guys stole-"

"I've heard," she interrupted. "But that's merely a history lesson of which I'm already familiar, not an answer to my question."

Remembering her exact wording, I said, "To destroy it."

She was silent for a moment. "How would you destroy it?"

"I'm not sure, but I need to find it before I can do anything."

"No," she said.

Her response seemed odd so I decided to change tracks. "Forgive me for being unfamiliar with this land, but I almost feel like I stepped through a portal and into Africa. The people are beautiful, but I never imagined anything like this even being possible after the wars. Where did y'all come from?"

The woman laughed, then rose to her feet. "I'm Queen Califa, fifth of my name, and the people you find so beautiful are the Niiji of Turtle Island. Where did we come from, you ask? You should ask that of yourself, because we've always been here."

I wasn't sure what to make of the Queen's last words, but I was confident I was getting nowhere. Back to the virus. "We could really use your help finding the weapon."

"There's no need," she said. "I'm already in possession of that which you seek. Now you may return home confident that your virus is safe."

Incredulous, I took a step toward Queen Califa.

Guards stepped toward me. A lot of them. From shadows and nooks and crannies.

"Stutenundud dudowæksnun." She walked in my direction. "He won't harm me."

As she closed the distance between us, I was able to get a clear look at her. The Queen was tall, maybe 5'9" or 5'10", with medium brown skin that held a red undertone. A golden head-dress covered long box braids that hung down her back, and two diamonds fell from the headdress down her forehead.

"I'm not leaving without that virus. It's not safe." Then I had a thought. "What happened to the two guys?"

"Do you question my competence? Do you think me irre-sponsible?" She waved a hand. "The weapon is mine and will remain in my care. Nothing more is to be said of it. You and your princess may enjoy my hospitality for as long as you please. The matter is now closed."

A young man with hazel eyes approached and bowed his head respectfully. "Please. Follow me to your quarters."

"But it-"

"Enough!" The Queen had fire in her eyes. "I have spoken."

We followed the young man out of the side of the room and up a few flights of stairs. As modern as this pyramid was I guessed they didn't believe in elevators. A hallway took us past a series of doors, and then each of us were directed to a specific door. Crush and Jael were assigned rooms on either side of Miranda, and I was at the end, next to Crush.

I dropped my pack to the floor and looked around. A king bed took up the center with twin nightstands on each side. Beneath the bed was a large Persian rug on top of blonde wood flooring. A dresser with a mirror on top sat next to a closet. And on the opposite wall was a bathroom.

Turning on the faucet, I splashed my face with water then looked into the mirror above the bathroom sink. I was tired and you could tell. We had traveled a long way and I was excited about sleeping in that bed. I couldn't wait to spread out across it and sink into its softness.

That bed was a condemned man's dream, and I was humbled that it was now my reality.

Knock. Knock. Knock.

There was an urgency in the taps.

After drying my face, I opened the door to Miranda rushing in. Her jaw was set, eyes tight.

"She won't give us the virus." Miranda paced, fists clenched. "Oooooh! She's such a bitch."

"Watch what you say," I cautioned. "This is her house. Never know who's listening."

"I don't care." She closed the distance between us. "Kill her. You've got to. That's the only way we're going to get that weapon and get back home. You *have* to kill her."

An ironic smile betrayed my face. "Now there's the Miranda I first met."

READING GROUP DISCUSSION QUESTIONS

1. Was Jason wrong for accepting the Gerent's mission?
2. How could one explain the connection between Brit and Jason, considering Jason's status as nephilim?
3. Is Brit solely motivated to help Jason because of their connection? What other reason might she have to aid in his journey?
4. Do you believe The One is a benevolent or evil diety? How does Vicar interpret The One's role in society?
5. Did you suspect Princess Miranda was the woman Jason had protected before his arrest?
6. Is Miranda a trustworthy character, considering her actions nearly got Jason executed?
7. What similarities do Jason and Nate share other than their angel ancestry?
8. Why does Vicar want Nana's help to control the dead?
9. Why did the Knights of Darkness react the Nate in a submissive manner in Hambrathia? Who might Nate be a descendent of?

10. What Role do you think King Nnendi and his kingdom will play in rest of the series?

ABOUT THE AUTHOR

At the age of 19, Kevin Macklin was arrested and sentenced to life without the possibility of parole. Over the past 20 years, he has experienced a tremendous amount of growth as a person. Growing up in the Washington DC area, Macklin was a constant presence at the local libraries and book stores. As he got older, he became a fan of the thriller genre, but noticed the blaring lack of heroes who looked like him with a similar background. So, he decided to write that character. Then, the characters and their stories just kept coming. Macklin looks forward to sharing his work with the world as he continues to work toward his freedom. Macklin is currently working on a petition in an effort to get a second chance at life. Please show your support by signing up for his newsletter at www.authorkevin.com

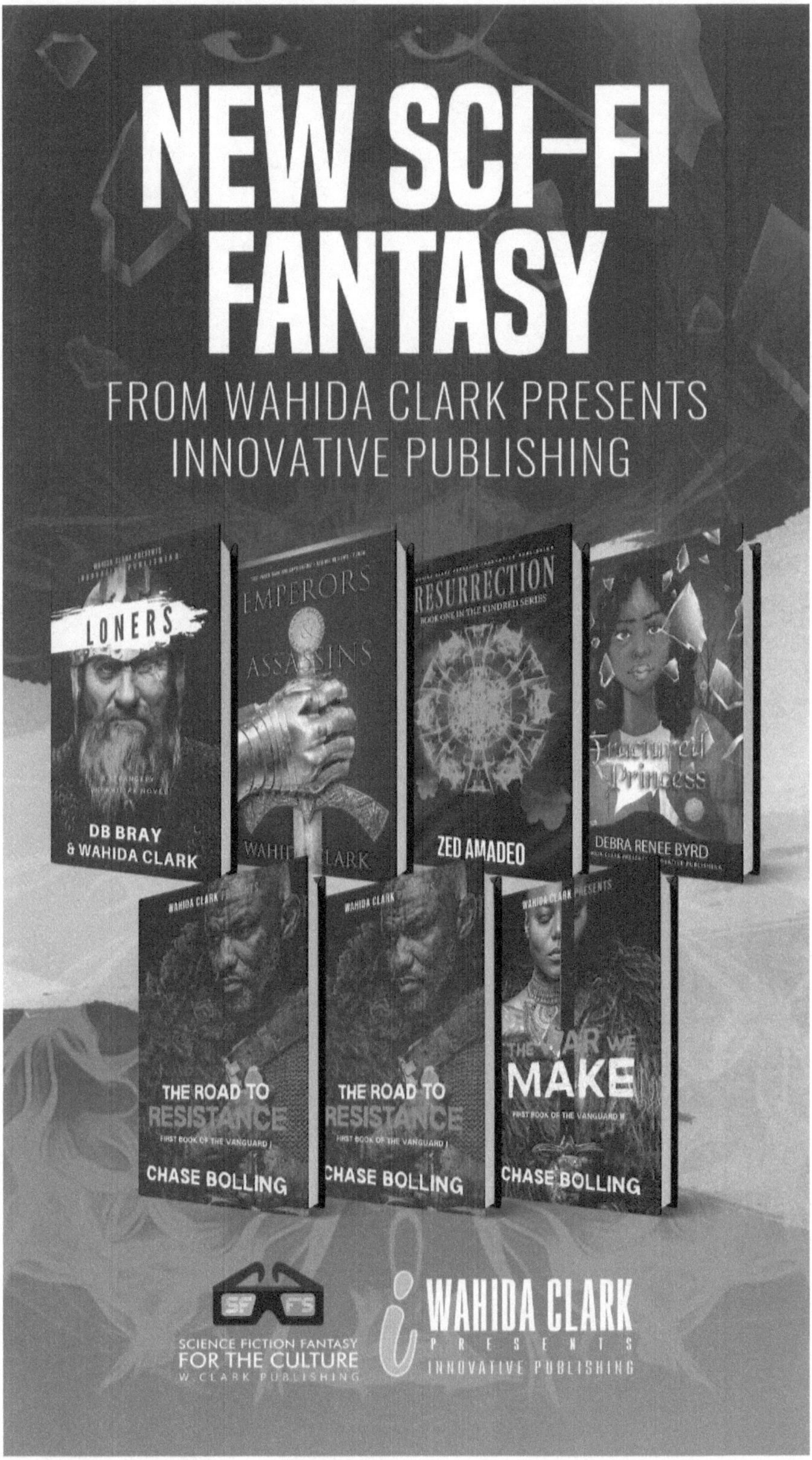
NEW SCI-FI
FANTASY
FROM WAHIDA CLARK PRESENTS
INNOVATIVE PUBLISHING
LONERS
DB BRAY
& WAHIDA CLARK
EMPERORS
ASSASSINS
RESURRECTION
BOOK ONE IN THE KINDRED SERIES
ZED AMADEO
Fractured Princess
DEBRA RENEE BYRD
THE ROAD TO
RESISTANCE
FIRST BOOK OF THE VANGUARD I
CHASE BOLLING
THE ROAD TO
RESISTANCE
FIRST BOOK OF THE VANGUARD I
CHASE BOLLING
MAKE
FIRST BOOK OF THE VANGUARD II
CHASE BOLLING
SF FS
SCIENCE FICTION FANTASY
FOR THE CULTURE
W. CLARK PUBLISHING
WAHIDA CLARK
PRESENTS
INNOVATIVE PUBLISHING

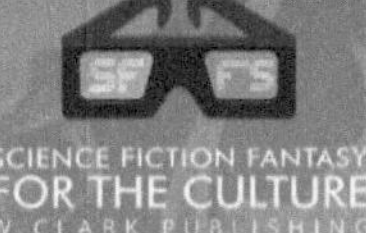

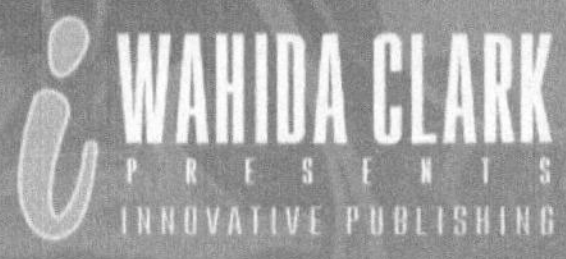